SPICED ORANGE SUSPICION

CLAIRE'S CANDLES

BOOK ELEVEN

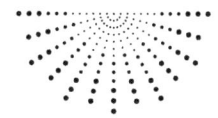

AGATHA FROST

PINK TREE PUBLISHING

Published by Pink Tree Publishing Limited in 2024

All characters and events in this publication, other than those clearly in the public domain, are fictitious and any resemblance to real persons, living or dead, is purely coincidental.

Copyright © Pink Tree Publishing Limited.

The moral right of the author has been asserted.

All rights reserved. This book or any portion thereof may not be reproduced or used in any manner whatsoever without the express written permission of the publisher except for the use of brief quotations in a book review.

For questions and comments about this book, please contact pinktreepublishing@gmail.com

www.pinktreepublishing.com
www.agathafrost.com

WANT TO BE KEPT UP TO DATE WITH AGATHA FROST RELEASES? *SIGN UP THE FREE NEWSLETTER!*

www.AgathaFrost.com

You can also follow **Agatha Frost** across social media. Search 'Agatha Frost' on:

Facebook
Twitter
Goodreads
Instagram

ALSO BY AGATHA FROST

Meadowfield Bookshop (NEW)

2. The Plot Thickens

1. **The Last Draft**

Claire's Candles

11. **Spiced Orange Suspicion**

10. **Double Espresso Deception**

9. **Frosted Plum Fears**

8. **Wildflower Worries**

7. **Candy Cane Conspiracies**

6. **Toffee Apple Torment**

5. **Fresh Linen Fraud**

4. **Rose Petal Revenge**

3. **Coconut Milk Casualty**

2. **Black Cherry Betrayal**

1. **Vanilla Bean Vengeance**

Peridale Cafe

32. **Lemon Drizzle Loathing**

31. **Sangria and Secrets**

30. Mince Pies and Madness
29. Pumpkins and Peril
28. Eton Mess and Enemies
27. Banana Bread and Betrayal
26. Carrot Cake and Concern
25. Marshmallows and Memories
24. Popcorn and Panic
23. Raspberry Lemonade and Ruin
22. Scones and Scandal
21. Profiteroles and Poison
20. Cocktails and Cowardice
19. Brownies and Bloodshed
18. Cheesecake and Confusion
17. Vegetables and Vengeance
16. Red Velvet and Revenge
15. Wedding Cake and Woes
14. Champagne and Catastrophes
13. Ice Cream and Incidents
12. Blueberry Muffins and Misfortune
11. Cupcakes and Casualties
10. Gingerbread and Ghosts
9. Birthday Cake and Bodies
8. Fruit Cake and Fear

7. **Macarons and Mayhem**

6. Espresso and Evil

5. Shortbread and Sorrow

4. Chocolate Cake and Chaos

3. Doughnuts and Deception

2. Lemonade and Lies

1. Pancakes and Corpses

Other

The Agatha Frost Winter Anthology

Peridale Cafe Book 1-10

Peridale Cafe Book 11-20

Claire's Candles Book 1-3

CHAPTER ONE

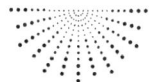

The spicy-sweet scent of orange, clove, and cinnamon filled Claire's Candles like a warm hug, as Claire Harris carefully adjusted the Star Candle of the Month display in the centre of the shop. Her latest festive spiced orange batch gleamed in its frosted jars, each label adorned with a hand-drawn illustration of a snow-dusted orange tree. She had agonised over the fragrance blend—bright citrus zest softened by a rich heart of nutmeg and cinnamon, finished with a base of creamy vanilla and a touch of cedarwood. It was, in her humble opinion, perfection.

"Careful with those," Damon called from the counter, his voice tinged with amusement. "You've been dropping candles all day."

"I'm fine!" Claire shot back, adjusting a precariously

perched jar. Her hands shook more with every passing hour. "I just want it to look *perfect* for the weekend rush."

"Since when did you care about perfect?" Damon's gaze flicked back to his phone, where he'd been glued most of the afternoon.

Claire rolled her eyes. "Since when did you care about Christmas shopping?"

"Always," he insisted, hastily turning the screen away when she tried to steal a glance. "You've got your candles, I've got my research."

"What kind of research, exactly?"

"Classified. Top secret." He grinned mischievously, tucking the phone into his pocket before she could get another look.

Claire sighed but let it drop. She was too distracted to care. Today wasn't just another day in her bustling little shop; it was *the* day. Finally, after months of renovations, delays, and too many sleepless nights to count, she and Ryan—and the kids—would be moving into their new home. Not just any home, either—Mrs Beaton's cottage on the very cul-de-sac where Claire and Ryan had grown up.

It felt like fate.

"Stop hovering and *go*," Damon said suddenly, jolting her from her thoughts.

Claire blinked. "What?"

"You've been pacing like a caged animal for hours. It's

driving me mad. Go to your new house. I'll finish up here."

"Damon, I can't just leave—"

"You can, and you will." He crossed his arms above his belly, giving her a pointed look over his glasses. "You're supposed to be unpacking boxes and arguing over curtain colours with Ryan. Seriously, Claire. You've earned this."

Claire hesitated, glancing around the shop. It wasn't that busy—just a few regulars browsing the discounted leftover summer scents. The shelves were stocked, the display was perfect, and Damon had managed on his own before.

"Fine," she said finally, grabbing her coat. "But call me if anything—"

"If anything explodes, catches fire, or requires a police intervention, you'll be the first to know," Damon said, cutting her off with a wink.

Claire laughed, slinging her bag over her shoulder and heading for the door. "Thanks, Damon. You're the best."

"I know," he called after her as the bell above the door jingled. "And I'll feed the cats!"

The cold December air hit her as she stepped outside, but Claire barely noticed. Her heart was already racing with excitement. Today, she wasn't just going to her new house—she was going *home*.

She stood at the edge of the sagging garden fence of the first house in the cul-de-sac, her breath rising in soft clouds against the frosty December air. A light dusting of snow had settled over the old, weathered street sign marking the lane that led back to Northash's centre. She brushed the flakes away with a knitted-gloved hand, revealing the faded name beneath. Birch Close.

To her, it was simply *the* cul-de-sac—the street where she'd grown up, forever overshadowed by the looming Warton Candle Factory. Its imposing presence had shaped every stage of her life: the distant hum of machinery in her childhood, the monotonous grind of her twenties and early thirties spent on the factory's looping conveyor belts. Now thirty-eight, running her very own candle shop in the village, she had left that life behind.

Birch Close itself had hardly changed. Claire's parents, Janet and Alan, still lived in their immaculately maintained home in the middle of the cul-de-sac, its garden as pristine as ever—even in the depths of winter. Next door, Ryan's childhood home sat quiet and vacant, its curtains drawn for years now. The six near-identical houses stood in their usual festive rivalry, each vying for the most elaborately decorated title. Strings of blinking lights crisscrossed eaves, inflatable Santas grinned from front gardens, and glowing reindeer grazed on patches of frost-bitten grass.

Except for one.

Mrs Beaton's old cottage—now Claire and Ryan's new home—stood apart, as shabby and forlorn as ever. It had always been the most neglected house in the cul-de-sac, its overgrown garden and peeling paint a stark contrast to its neighbours' pristine facades.

For years, the cottage had been overrun by Mrs Beaton's army of cats—just one part of the chaotic hoard she'd amassed over the decades. The cats had since found better homes, Janet and Claire had gutted the place inside and out, and Mrs Beaton was now in a residential home down in the Cotswolds where she could be properly cared for in her old age.

Months of work had brought the house closer to being liveable, but it was still far from finished. Scaffolding clung to the right side like a steel skeleton, while a loose blue tarpaulin flapped noisily in the brisk wind, its edges snapping against the cold air.

Claire squeezed Ryan's hand, searching for a flicker of shared excitement. Instead, his distant expression made her squeeze harder.

"The builders will be back in the New Year once the weather warms up," Ryan assured her, though the slight tremor in his voice suggested he was trying to convince himself as much as her. "They said it's perfectly liveable for now, even without a proper kitchen."

"We'll make it work," Claire replied, injecting as much

cheer as possible—mainly for the kids' sake. "It'll be like camping."

Not that they had much choice—time had forced their hand.

Ryan hadn't renewed the tenancy on his terraced house, which he'd rented since returning to Northash after years abroad. For weeks, they'd been crammed into the tiny flat above the candle shop—a space overtaken by the chaos of her busiest business year yet. Boxes stacked in every corner left little room for everyday life. Weeks of living on top of one another had pushed them all to the edge. They were desperate for change, even if their 'before Christmas' move-in deadline now meant settling into an unfinished house.

Amelia and Hugo bounded over on the thin layer of snow still clinging to the road after the recent storm. Hugo's cheeks glowed as red as Santa's coat, his grin wide as he cradled a precarious mound of snowballs in his arms. Amelia, taller, willowier—and looking more like Ryan every day—elbowed him gently.

"I'm getting the biggest room," Amelia declared, her voice carrying to the house. "I deserve it."

"*Daaad*, Amelia said I'd be living under the stairs!"

"And you believed me," Amelia teased, tossing a snowball at her brother.

It missed, smacking into the gate with a satisfying

thump. The gate swung open with a slow, protesting creak.

Ryan laughed, crouching to adjust Hugo's knitted hat, tugging it back up from where it had slipped over his eyes.

"You won't be under the stairs," he said gently. "Unless you want to be. Then we'll make it as cosy as possible."

"I'd prefer a downstairs bathroom in there," Claire added, winking at Hugo before giving Amelia a sterner look. "Stop winding up your brother. And don't you *dare* throw that—"

Amelia's snowball hit Claire square in the stomach. The twelve-year-old froze, her face flushing with panic as if expecting to be grounded. But one perk of being the unofficial stepmother—Claire and Ryan were undecided on marriage—was not having to play the bad cop.

Grinning, Claire grabbed a handful of snow from the street sign and hurled it back. Her aim was no better than Amelia's. The snowball sailed into the neighbour's garden, knocking over a festive gnome fishing in their frozen water feature.

Carol Hodgkinson, ever the nosy neighbour, twitched the curtains. Claire turned away, brushing snow from her hands.

"There's enough space for *everyone* to have a big room," she said, steering the conversation away from their audience. "And we'll finally have a proper craft space—half for my candles, half for your paintings."

Ryan gave her hand a brief squeeze, his lips curving into a faint smile.

"About that," he began, suddenly serious. "There's something I wanted to talk to you about over dinner. Painting-related." But before he could continue, his narrowing gaze shifted to the house. "I think I just saw movement. Inside."

Claire followed his line of sight, frowning at the upper windows. The panes were still covered by yellowed newspaper, but the wind caught one corner, seeping through the single-pane windows and flapping it against the glass. She shivered.

"Probably nothing," she said.

But a muffled crash from inside sent her heart racing.

Both Claire and Ryan froze.

"What was that?" Amelia asked, craning her neck to peer past them. "Burglars?"

"There's nothing to steal," Hugo replied.

"There *is*!" Amelia shot back, sticking out her tongue. "I packed all *your* stuff and even left a note for the burglars so they'd know what to steal."

"Daaaaaad."

"Off to Granny and Pops' house," Ryan said quickly, too focused on the upstairs windows to play around. "Ask nicely, and they might make you a hot chocolate."

"But—"

"Go. Now."

With a pointed look from Claire, the children ran, snow forgotten. Hugo tripped over his scarf as Amelia dragged him along. Janet's front door creaked open before they reached it, her head poking out, equal parts curious and concerned. Carol wasn't the only one who enjoyed curtain twitching. Ryan waited until Janet ushered the children inside before moving towards the house.

"It's probably one of Mrs Beaton's old cats," Claire suggested, though her voice wavered. "Snuck back in somehow?"

Ryan wasn't listening. He was already reaching for the handle when the door burst open with such force that he stumbled back.

A young man with shaggy blond hair, dishevelled and wild-eyed, tumbled out onto the front step. He hit the frozen ground hard, clutching a rucksack to his chest. Scrambling to his feet, he shot Ryan a panicked glare before bolting past them. He tripped over the old gate, ripping it clean off the rotting hinges, vanishing into the night.

"Ryan, no!" Claire grabbed his arm. "Let him go."

"But—"

"Let's see what's inside first."

The old house loomed behind them, its door yawning

open, daring them to enter. The carpets had been ripped up, the bare walls covered in fresh plaster, and from the landing upstairs, a faint light.

A woman with purple hair appeared at the top of the stairs, her voice sharp and frantic. "*Ricky*! Come back!"

The woman froze when her eyes landed on Claire and Ryan. Without another word, she turned and ran, her heavy footsteps echoing on the uncarpeted landing.

"Jodie!" the purple-haired girl cried. "There's *people*!"

"Who's Jodie?" Ryan stepped in front of Claire. "Stay here."

"Fat chance!" she replied, slipping past him before he could stop her. "I'm not standing outside while you play hero. You might have the muscles, but I can hold my own."

They hurried up the creaky staircase together, their footsteps echoing in the hollow silence of the house. The air was damp and musty, carrying the sharp tang of the cold. Before they reached the landing, a woman stepped out of the shadows.

Jodie was bundled in layers of thick clothing—a shabby coat over a bulky jumper, with a scarf wrapped snugly around her neck. A thin scar traced her right cheek, running from her ear to the corner of her lips. Claire recognised the woman—she'd seen her slumped on benches near the clock tower opposite the candle shop, watching the world with a detached, almost expectant stare. More than once, Claire had overheard Detective Inspector Harry Ramsbottom trying to move her along. Claire guessed she was in her late thirties.

"Who are you?" Jodie demanded, her eyes darting warily between Claire and Ryan.

"Who are *we*?" Claire cried, her temper flaring. "Who are *you*? This is our house."

"You need to leave," Ryan ordered.

Jodie's lips curled into a smug grin. "*We* live here now, mate. Squatters' rights. You've heard of them, yeah?"

Claire's mouth fell open in disbelief, but another figure emerged from the shadows behind Jodie before she could respond.

This man was broad and older, his posture radiating a tense, defensive energy. Deep lines etched his face, and his sharp, watchful eyes gave him the air of someone well-acquainted with confrontation. He shot Jodie a scathing glance.

"Speak for yourself," he muttered gruffly. "This isn't permanent for all of us."

"Zip it, Stuart," Jodie shot back.

Claire's stomach tightened. Whoever these people were, they weren't a united front.

"You need to go," Ryan repeated, his voice firm. "We're supposed to be moving in. We've got two kids, and—"

"*Legally*, we don't *need* to go anywhere," Jodie interrupted, her smirk widening as she folded her arms.

"Not until you've got the proper paperwork. Unless you want to drag me out kicking and screaming, muscle princess?"

She reached out and patted Ryan's arm, making him flinch backwards.

"Yeah, I didn't think so. You gym bunnies are all the same." Jodie's grin stretched wider. "You know it's rude to turn up to a housewarming empty-handed, right?"

Claire's gaze shifted past Jodie, drawn by a flicker of movement. The young woman who'd alerted Jodie darted from one of the rear bedrooms, looking barely twenty-five. Her wide, nervous eyes glinted in the dim light, and her purple-dyed hair hung limp, clearly in need of a wash.

Following close behind was another figure—a silent, older woman swathed in more layers than anyone else. Her expression was hard to read, but her eyes carried the weight of someone who had seen too much.

These weren't just random intruders—they were living here, hiding in the back bedrooms away from the street. It couldn't have been more than a few days—she and Ryan had been here over the weekend, installing new carpet in the craft room.

"Merry Christmas, by the way," Jodie said, giving them a double thumbs-up as she backed away. "You've done a great job with this place already. Shame you didn't *lock* the back door."

Stuart offered a faintly apologetic smile but didn't linger. Stuart, the young woman, and the older woman trailed after Jodie into the largest bedroom. The door slammed shut, followed by the unmistakable scrape of something heavy being dragged across the floor, sealing them in and keeping Claire and Ryan out of *their* bedroom.

"This can't be happening," Claire whispered, turning to Ryan.

He slipped an arm around her shoulders, pulling her close.

"We'll sort it," he said softly. "Somehow, we'll fix this."

She wanted to laugh. A sharp, bitter laugh at how absurd it all was. Between running her shop, juggling the kids, the endless stress of modernising the old house on a tight budget, and now this—dealing with a group of strangers claiming squatters' rights—she didn't know if she had the energy for one more complication.

But here it was—the kind of complication she could never have seen coming. And, like it or not, they would have to face it head-on.

CHAPTER TWO

Claire shivered in the stripped-out kitchen, where the bare walls seemed to magnify every sound: the groan of the wind outside, the muffled thuds from upstairs, and her father's weary sighs as he leaned against his cane. She sat at the rickety folding table, her finger idly tracing a chip in its worn surface.

This wasn't how she'd imagined the start of their new life. She'd been prepared for chaos—no proper kitchen, a freezer stuffed with microwave meals, and endlessly shaking the air fryer basket. But it was supposed to be *their* chaos. Not this.

Alan, her father, a stout man who shared Claire's 'Harris figure', leaned against the counter with his phone in hand, tapping out messages to old colleagues. His lined face was stern, but there was a fire of his old policing determination in his tired eyes. He glanced up as Ryan came in, carrying three steaming mugs from across the cul-de-sac.

"You're a good lad," Alan said, accepting the mug with both hands.

"Any luck?" Ryan asked as he sat down beside Claire, his tone cautious but hopeful.

"DI Ramsbottom's not picking up," Alan replied, sucking air through his teeth as he scrolled through his phone. "But I'm waiting on a call back from the old desk sergeant. I'll tell you this: they don't have a legal leg to stand on. Squatting like this became a criminal offence when I still had my badge, and that's going back some years now."

"They're counting on us not checking," Ryan said, looking up to the ceiling as though he could glare through the floorboards.

"We'll figure it out." Claire reached out, resting a calming hand on his arm. "It's just going to take some time."

Ryan shook his head, his jaw tightening. "It's just not right."

Before Claire could agree, the faint shuffle of footsteps in the hall caught her attention. A moment later, the younger woman with purple hair appeared in the doorway, hesitating just long enough to let the older woman step in beside her.

The younger woman kept her arms folded tightly across her duffle coat, her eyes fixed anywhere but on the three of them. The older woman, on the other hand, stood tall, her weathered face calm but hardened.

Ryan stood, nodding his recognition at the younger woman.

"It's Lucy, isn't it?" he asked. "I thought that was you. You used to manage the gallery down by the café."

Lucy flinched. "I don't want to talk about it."

"And she doesn't have to," the older woman cut in, her tone protective but even. Her gaze swept over the room before settling on Alan. "We've all got stories. I was a seamstress," she continued. "Then I broke my wrist. Couldn't work after that, and before I knew it, I'd lost everything. It happens fast, especially when you don't have much to start with. You already know her name, so I'm Maria."

Alan shifted, leaning heavier on his cane, the creak of its rubber base loud against the exposed floorboards.

"I'm sorry to hear about your circumstances," he said. "I'm guessing you're about my age?"

"Must be," Maria agreed. "You're a copper, aren't you?"

"I was," Alan said, stiffening at the accusation in her tone. "Did I ever arrest you?"

Maria frowned, unamused. "*No*. And I never was arrested. But I made it my business to know the local fuzz. Good to know who to avoid."

"Depending on the officer, not the worst idea," he said, still offering her a smile. "Maria, I'll level with you. Legally, you've got no right to be here. You could all be arrested once we prove Claire and Ryan own this house. Six months in prison. Fines in the thousands."

"*No*," Lucy whispered, her voice trembling as the colour drained from her face. "You can't—"

"Please, don't let it come to that," Maria cut in, her voice laced with quiet desperation. "We've got nothing— barely two pennies to rub together. We're not causing any harm, and we're not making a mess. But we've got nowhere else to go."

"Where did you come from?" Claire asked, her curiosity genuine.

"Here and there." Maria shrugged, her guarded eyes betraying a lack of trust. "If we had anywhere else to go, anyone to turn to, we would. We rely on each other and the kindness of strangers. There's no honour in this life. No dignity. I never had children, and I was an only child. Lucy's parents passed away years ago."

"The council—" Alan began.

"Do you know how hard it is to deal with *the system* without a fixed address?" Maria snapped, exhaustion sharpening her words. "Please, spare us the lecture. We've *heard* it. Like I said, we're not making a mess, and we don't stay in one place for long. For obvious reasons."

A shadow loomed in the doorway. Jodie sauntered in, her smirk firmly in place.

"Yeah," she echoed, her mocking tone cutting as she folded her arms and leaned lazily against the doorframe. "Nowhere to go. What are you going to do—kick us out into the snow? Watch us freeze to death? At Christmas?" She arched her brows. "You want *that* on your conscience?"

Claire glanced at Ryan, then back at Jodie. She forced herself to remain composed, unwilling to give her the satisfaction of a reaction. But her smugness was getting under Claire's skin. Jodie was either their ringleader or enjoyed acting like it. Either way, Claire already couldn't stand the sight of her.

"No, we won't," Claire said, matching her cold stare. "You have one night."

Stuart appeared at the bottom of the stairs, his heavy boots thudding against the floorboards.

"The only reason I'm in this mess is *you*," he muttered, jerking a thumb towards Jodie. "I want my money."

"And you'll get it," Jodie snapped, her smirk faltering for the first time. "Haven't I told you I'll get it? Don't worry about it. Not in front of our kind guests."

Claire's stomach twisted as Jodie's smarmy grin returned. Beneath the table, Ryan's hand settled on her knee. She hadn't even realised her fists were clenched, but as she forced them to relax, she reminded herself not to let Jodie see she was getting to her. The woman was enjoying this far too much—relishing every moment of the power she held.

"If I had my way," Ryan said, his voice steady but clipped, "I'd call the police right now. I'm sorry, but I would."

"Tomorrow morning," Claire said firmly. "*One* night. Then you all need to figure out your next moves."

"We will." Maria nodded, her shoulders relaxing. "Thank you."

Lucy lingered, shifting awkwardly behind Maria, as if trying to make herself invisible. She had stayed silent through the entire interaction, offering nothing. But as she turned, her gaze flicked to Ryan and lingered.

"You've had a few paintings in the gallery," she said. "You have a good eye."

Ryan's cheeks flushed, and he glanced down, a small, self-conscious smile forming.

"Thank you. I've sold a few." He noticed a guitar propped by the fridge. "Is that yours? I think I've heard someone playing guitar at the gallery before."

"It's Ricky's," Lucy replied, wringing her hands. Her voice dropped as she added, "He ran off earlier. He looks after us. Keeps us going." She noticed Jodie, who stood waiting for her at the bottom of the stairs, arms crossed. "But he's gone now," she murmured before retreating upstairs.

Jodie followed, shooting a final pleased grin over her shoulder before slamming the door to Claire and Ryan's future bedroom.

"That was decent of you, little one," Alan said, taking a few cautious steps on the uneven floor. His cane tapped softly against the boards as he steadied himself. "But you know, I could still call Harry Ramsbottom and have the lot of them in cells by midnight. Just say the word."

"Jodie was right." Claire stood by the window as the snow fell in thick, heavy flakes, blanketing the garden. "We're not going to see them freeze. Not tonight."

"You can stay with your mother and me tonight. Beds are already made up." Alan paused, a faint glimmer of mischief in his eyes. "Your mum thought you'd chicken out of living here like this."

Claire gave him a tired smile. "I wouldn't. But now?" She glanced over her shoulder at Ryan, her voice quiet as she added, "Let's go. I don't want to be here."

CHAPTER THREE

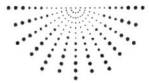

The cold nipped at Claire's nose as she and Ryan walked away from 1 Birch Close, crossing the cul-de-sac. Alan trailed a step behind, his cane crunching against the snow-dusted pavement. The flakes were falling faster now, settling on her scarf and melting on her nose. She tugged her coat tighter, her thoughts spinning with the shock of the intruders.

Next door, Carol and Kris Hodgkinson stood on their doorstep, wrapped in plush dressing gowns. Carol's was a pale pink that might have been elegant if not paired with her perpetually sour expression.

"*Squatters?*" Carol's voice cut through the quiet night like a scythe. She shook her head, her glossy curls bouncing with exaggerated indignation. "Seriously, Claire? Are you trying to drag down our property values?

Mrs Beaton should never have given you that house at such a discount. You clearly can't afford to secure it."

Claire stopped mid-step, biting back the retort forming on her tongue. But Ryan's steadying hand on her elbow kept her grounded.

"I didn't do it on purpose," she called back, her voice weary despite the sharpness she'd intended. "Goodnight, Carol."

"That's *Mrs Hodgkinson* to you!"

"Leave it, Carol," Kris sighed, rubbing a hand over his face. He looked resigned, as though he'd long since accepted his role as buffer to his wife's tirades. "The velvetiser should have our hot chocolates ready by now."

Carol shot Claire one last glare before storming inside, slamming the door behind her with enough force to dislodge the pinecone wreath. It tumbled to the ground with a muted thud, lying in the snow like a forgotten afterthought.

"Not the best start with the new neighbours," Ryan said.

"You know what Carol and Kris are like," Alan called.

"Been the same since we were kids," Claire said, stepping closer. "It was never going to be cups of sugar over the fence, was it?" She nodded towards numbers 5 and 6 across the cul-de-sac. "Who lives there these days, Dad?"

"A lovely couple with two kids at number 5—the

Chopra family," he replied. "But they keep themselves to themselves. And number 6? You'll remember Stephen Smith, a retired army officer. Lost his wife a few years ago, poor man. We don't see much of him anymore." He paused, then added, "Number 3's still empty. A property company snapped it up—they're probably waiting for the market to pick up before they flog it."

By the time they reached her parents' house, Claire's fingers were numb, and the thought of warmth—real, unrelenting warmth—felt like a distant dream. Her childhood home glowed like something out of a lifestyle magazine. Twinkling silver lights framed the windows, and inside, every surface shimmered with rose-gold decorations. Dancing elf ornaments swayed from the mantelpiece, festive candles from Claire's shop flickered on the shelves, and wreaths and tinsel wrapped anything that could hold them.

She stepped inside and inhaled a cloying mix of scents. Last year's frosted plum candle mingled with this year's spiced orange variety. The sweetness made her stomach turn.

Kicking off her boots in the hallway, she heard the faint clink of mugs and the low hum of the kettle from the kitchen.

"Squatters, Claire?" Janet's voice carried out. Though less cutting, it had the same grating quality as Carol's accusation. "*Really?*"

"I'm not in the mood, Mother. I had a busy Friday shift at the shop, and Ryan's been working at the gym all day."

"As have I," Janet replied, appearing in the doorway with a tray of hot chocolates topped with squirty cream and a sprinkle of gold dust. "My cleaning company doesn't run itself, you know. Lancashire would be a much grimier place without Janet's Angels watching over it."

She swept into the sitting room and set the tray on the coffee table, the rich aroma of chocolate filling the room.

"Still, I'll give your house a top-to-bottom clean once they've moved on."

"*If* they move on," Ryan said, sinking onto the sofa with a sigh.

"They will," Alan said firmly, lowering himself into his armchair by the fire with a groan. "Claire showed them some kindness. They'd be fools to ignore it."

Claire sat beside Ryan and cupped one of the mugs in her hands, letting the warmth seep into her frozen fingers. Still, the knot in her chest refused to loosen.

"I hope you're right," she said quietly, leaning back against the cushions.

But as she stared out the window, watching the snow fall heavier and faster, Claire couldn't help but wonder if kindness would be enough.

Later that night, Claire crossed the cul-de-sac alone. At the broken gate, she hesitated. Light poured from the sitting room window, pooling on the overgrown grass. She wasn't sure what she was hoping for—laughter, arguments, any sign of life—but the stillness was broken only by the muted strum of a guitar. The sound wasn't cheerful. Just three melancholy chords, repeated over and over, as if the musician couldn't decide how to move forward.

She slipped closer, keeping to the shadows of the scaffolding. Inside, the squatters were moving about like they owned the place. A man with a battered guitar—Ricky, who'd sprinted away earlier—sat perched on the arm of her sofa, plucking at the strings. The sagging couch had been a gift from her Granny Greta's old back bedroom.

Lucy was bowed over a sketchbook in the corner, her face twisted in concentration as she scribbled. Charcoal smudged her fingers, the black streaks stark against her pale skin. Occasionally, she glanced at Ricky, muttering something Claire couldn't hear.

By the fireplace, Jodie stood, surveying the room like a queen inspecting her court. She leaned against the mantel, a steaming mug in hand. She said something to Lucy; whatever it was, it made her snap her charcoal down. She left the room and went through to the back.

Stuart was in the kitchen, a knife scratching into the

surface of the table Claire had dragged in just yesterday, salvaged from a skip in the square. His shoulders flinched at Jodie's laughter, but he stayed silent, his focus unbroken.

In the corner, Maria sat alone, quietly darning a pair of socks with a needle and thread.

Claire stepped back, the frozen grass crunching under her slippers. These were the people she was supposed to evict? They looked like a disjointed improvisation troupe, all mismatched energy and friction—like jagged stones grinding together, brittle and dangerous, waiting for the slightest pressure to crack. These people had been around each other for far too long.

And snap, they did.

"Right, *out*!" Jodie cried out of nowhere. "I've kicked you out once tonight, and I let you back in from the goodness of my heart to collect your guitar, but I'm sick of hearing your ear-piercing plucking."

"Leave him alone," Stuart muttered.

"Yeah," Maria echoed.

"Nah, it's alright," Ricky said, ditching his guitar. "I'll go out into the night and freeze, just like you want, Jodie. You're all welcome to come with me." He paused by the sitting room door, deflated. "Nah, I didn't think so."

Before she crossed Ricky's path again, Claire crept around the back of the house. The wild, overgrown garden loomed ahead, its tangle of brambles and weeds glowing faintly under the moonlight.

At the edge of the garden, she spotted Lucy crouched near the gnarled remains of an old apple tree. Her shoulders trembled as she sobbed into her hands.

"I *hate* her," Lucy muttered, her voice ragged and barely audible over the distant wind. "I *hate* her. I *hate* her. I *hate* her."

Claire hesitated, her heart lurching at the rawness in Lucy's voice. Then, stepping closer, she broke the silence. "Lucy? Are you alright?"

Lucy's head jerked up, her pale face streaked with tears, her charcoal-stained fingers trembling as she clutched them together. She shook her head quickly, a small, sharp motion, but didn't speak.

Claire opened her mouth to say something more, but the sharp rap of knuckles against glass made her jump. She spun towards the house and saw Jodie glaring out at them from the sitting room window. Her eyes were cold, her lips curled in disdain.

"Lucy, *in*," Jodie barked.

Lucy shot to her feet without a word and trudged back to the house, her head bowed low. Claire watched her go, frustration bubbling in her chest.

Alone in the garden, Claire exhaled a shaky breath. What had she been hoping to find? That the squatters had simply vanished into the night? That they'd resolved their strange, simmering conflicts and gone somewhere else?

Her gaze drifted beyond the garden wall to the conservatory next door. Carol and Kris were inside, their newly built addition illuminated by soft golden candlelight. But the scene inside was far from cosy.

Carol's arms were flung wide in exasperation, her face flushed as she argued with Kris. He was gesturing just as wildly, his mouth moving in angry, silent bursts. Then, without warning, Carol snatched a potted poinsettia from the table and hurled it at the wall. The crimson petals exploded in a dramatic splash of colour against the glass.

Peering over the garden fence, Claire held her breath. Kris stared at Carol, his expression cold and incredulous. He shook his head, barked a sharp laugh, and walked away, disappearing into the house. A door slammed seconds later, rattling the conservatory windows.

The cul-de-sac felt on the verge of imploding.

Claire's gaze lingered on Carol, who had crumpled into a wicker chair, her face buried in her hands as she sobbed. For a fleeting moment, Claire considered going over to check on her, but the idea withered. She'd known Carol for years, and that wouldn't end well. Not tonight.

Creeping back down the side of the house, she rounded the corner and froze. Stuart stood out front, leaning against the scaffolding with a cigarette glowing between his fingers.

"Watch your back," he said, his voice low and gravelly.

Claire stiffened. "Excuse me?"

"It's late. A little too dark for you to be wandering around alone," he replied, taking a slow drag. "Go back to your warm bed."

She considered telling him that this was the one place in the whole village she'd always felt safe. But tonight, that wouldn't be true.

As she turned away from Stuart, Claire spotted Ricky standing near the mouth of the lane, his head tipped back as he stared up at the sky. His breath billowed in frosty clouds hanging in the still air. He seemed frozen in place, a statue against the winter night. Then, without warning, he let out a raw, piercing scream—a sound that shattered the silence and echoed through the cul-de-sac.

Curtains twitched at numbers 5 and 6, faint shapes moving behind the frosted glass.

Claire hesitated before stepping closer. "Where are you going to go?" she asked softly.

Ricky spun to face her. "Like *you* care!"

But she did.

"My parents won't let you into the house, but my dad has a shed at the bottom of the garden. There's a heater in there."

Ricky's glare eased, and for a fleeting moment, Claire

thought he might agree. But then his head dropped, and he turned away, plodding off down the lane without another word.

Claire watched him go, his figure shrinking into the darkness, before finally returning to her parents' house.

"Where've you been?" her mother asked, emerging from the downstairs bathroom in a cloud of cinnamon air freshener.

"Out."

"You went over *there*, didn't you?" she asked, shaking her head. "Don't deny it. Your cheeks are almost purple from the cold. You're trying to get yourself killed, aren't you?"

"Yes, Mother," she replied flatly, arching a brow. "That's *exactly* it."

"Don't get lippy, Claire."

"Don't be ridiculous, Mother," she said, climbing the stairs. "I appreciate you letting us stay, but let's not do this, okay? We're far too old for the bickering mother-daughter act."

"Hmm," Janet grumbled, watching Claire go. "You're not too old to be grounded."

"I'm thirty-eight, Mother!"

"You're basically a child until you're forty!" Janet called after her. "And you're welcome for the hot water bottle I slipped under your pillow!"

The house was still. Her parents had gone to bed over an hour ago, their synchronised snores now rumbling through the walls. Claire padded down the hall, her slippers muffling her steps against the thick carpet, and nudged the door to the second guest bedroom open.

A soft glow bled out from under the duvet where Hugo was still awake, hunched over his Nintendo Switch.

She leaned against the doorframe, smiling to herself. Amelia was fast asleep in the bed beside him, her strawberry-blonde hair splayed across the pillow like a halo. Hugo, oblivious to her presence, mashed buttons on his console, his face bathed in the blue-white glow of the screen.

"You know," Claire whispered, stepping inside, "I used to do the same thing with my Gameboy."

Hugo jumped, nearly dropping the Switch in his surprise. He shot her a sheepish look before trying to hide the console under the duvet.

"Sorry, Claire."

Claire perched on the edge of the bed, smoothing the blanket over his legs.

"I used to play under the covers too—until I lost mine on the school bus."

"What happened?" he asked, lowering the console, curiosity winning out.

"Your dad saved up and bought me another at a car boot sale," she said, her smile soft with the memory. "The screen only half worked, but I treasured it."

Hugo grinned. "Dad's cool like that."

"Yeah," she agreed, brushing a stray lock of hair back from his forehead. "He is." She glanced at the glowing screen. "Ten more minutes, and then lights off. Promise?"

"Promise," Hugo replied with a nod, though she could already tell ten minutes might stretch closer to twenty. As she stood and turned to leave, his voice stopped her. "Claire?"

"Yes, love?"

"Are we ever going to move into the new house?"

Her hand paused on the doorknob. She turned back, forcing a reassuring smile.

"I promise we will."

She hoped it was a promise she could keep.

HER OLD BEDROOM HADN'T CHANGED MUCH. THE wallpaper had been updated countless times, but the slightly wobbly dressing table—where she'd mixed her first candle scents—still stood in its usual spot. Aside from the elliptical machine tucked in the corner, the room was hotel-ready, a habit of her mother's for drop-of-the-hat guests. Claire was grateful for it tonight.

Through the window, the dark hill stretched out as it always had beyond Ian Barton's farm, the old candle factory perched at its crest.

Ryan stood by the window in his lounge pants, his t-shirt folded neatly over a chair. Claire, already snug in her fluffy penguin pyjamas—dug out from under the Christmas tree by her mother and gifted with a pointed 'to cheer you up'—climbed into bed with a sigh, pulling back the covers. Domino and Sid, her cats, were curled at the foot of the bed, content and warm. Her dad had driven her back to the flat earlier to collect them, and their presence made everything feel a little more normal.

"If they're not gone tomorrow," Ryan said, still staring out into the night, "I'm calling the police myself."

"One more bump," Claire murmured, lying back against the pillows. The hot water bottle was still toasty underneath. "It was only a few years ago I was stuck here. Working at the factory, no future, just this room and my cats."

She stopped, unwilling to follow the thought any further. Even with squatters in their new home, life was better now—so much better. She had her candle shop, Ryan, the kids, and a future she could finally picture. But something from earlier in the night lingered, unfinished in her mind.

"What were you trying to tell me?" she asked, pulling

back the covers on his side. "Before we were interrupted by our houseguests."

"It's not important." He hesitated, then crossed the room to join her, sliding under the covers and pulling her close. "Not tonight."

"It sounded important." Claire tilted her head, her eyes searching his face. "Painting-related, you said."

He sighed, considering. "I was offered a new job. At the gallery."

"Ryan, that's amazing!" Her voice brightened, and she pushed herself up slightly. "Are you thinking of taking it?"

"They're looking for a manager, presumably because Lucy left," he said with uncertainty. "I dropped off a painting earlier today—they sold the one of the observatory at Starfall Park—and the owner mentioned he'd had to fire her a few months ago and had been looking for someone since."

"Do you know why?"

"No. I should've asked."

"You weren't to know," she said, brushing his arm with her fingers. "But Ryan, that's brilliant. You'd be around art all day."

"It'd be nicer than the gym," he admitted, his voice softening. "But the money's worse. And there's no guarantee of hours."

She studied him in the dim light of the bedside lamp,

the shadow of doubt cast over his handsome face. Resting her head against his chest, she let the steady thud of his heartbeat ground her. Ryan had always been like this—hesitant, cautious with big decisions. And she understood. She'd been stuck herself too many times before, afraid to take that leap.

"You know," she murmured, snuggling closer, "if you didn't *want* to take it, we wouldn't be having this conversation."

"I know, it's just the *timing*."

"When is the timing ever right?"

"Good point," he admitted with a low chuckle. "But right now, it's chaos. And chaos has a way of getting worse before it gets better."

"It won't," she said. "Besides, I promised Hugo we'd be moving in, and I don't intend to break that promise."

She hesitated, the dreaded deadline she'd been holding onto hovering on the tip of her tongue. The builders had promised Christmas months ago, only to miss it by a mile. But even now, the thought of that day—of the house finally ready—made her chest ache with longing.

"I'll do whatever it takes to make sure we're all in *our* home on Christmas morning," she stated. "The tree, the presents, the turkey—"

"*I'll* cook the turkey," Ryan cut in, his grin playful. "No offence."

She swatted him, their laughter breaking the tension. He kissed her, pulling her close, their shared warmth a quiet balm against the night's chill. Domino stretched and meowed, crawling up to perch on the pillows above their heads like a watchful guardian. Sid stayed by the warmth of their feet.

"One night," Claire whispered, her voice fading as her eyes closed. "Our new life starts tomorrow."

CHAPTER FOUR

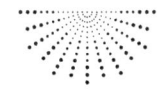

As the sun struggled to pierce the grey morning gloom, Claire waited outside her shop, buried deep in her puffa jacket. She surveyed the freshly arranged spiced orange display in the window—her latest Star Candle of the Month. She'd perfected it on just the third iteration of testers.

The soft glow of dancing fairy lights framed the display, casting a warm golden hue over the deep amber and rustic red candles nestled in their ornate jars. With its delicate watercolour painting of an orange, the label was Ryan's creation—more enticing than any of her previous plain-text designs. Around the tiers, dried orange slices, cinnamon sticks, and sprigs of holly were arranged with care.

Claire rubbed her hands together against the crisp

morning air, the satisfaction of her work warming her more than the feeble December sun. The display was simple, but she liked its understated elegance. She'd never have described herself as elegant, but years of arranging displays had taught her what she did and didn't like.

Unlike the other shops in Northash's square—decked out with baubles, Santa hats, and colourful flashing lights—her display didn't shout *'It's Christmas!'* Instead, it invited you to curl up in your fluffiest jumper with a steaming mug of something warm.

She'd imagined lighting the first cured jar—a treat she'd set aside for their first night in the new house—by now.

Claire glanced at her watch. Damon was late. Again. His flat was only a few doors down, above Marley's Café, but punctuality had never been his strong suit. Her gaze drifted to the lane leading towards the cul-de-sac.

Were her unwanted houseguests still there? Had they packed up and moved on, or were they digging in their heels?

The sharp screech of brakes jolted her from her thoughts. A delivery van came to an uneasy halt in front of the shop, skidding against the fluffy snow settling over the slush. It narrowly avoided Damon, who was dashing across the road, his scarf—modelled after Tom Baker's Doctor in *Doctor Who*, or so he'd proudly informed her—trailing behind him like a cape.

"Watch where you're going!" the driver called through the open window.

"Same to you!" Damon shot back cheerfully, unfazed as he jogged to Claire's side.

The driver began unloading the new empty jars so they could start their spring collection, dropping the boxes with unnecessary force. Damon didn't seem to notice.

"Sorry I'm late," he said, his breath clouding the air. "Slept through my alarm. You can blame *Dawn Ship 2: Requiem* for keeping me up. Got a bit carried away."

Claire suppressed a smile. "New game?"

"Expansion pack." Damon's face lit up as he launched into an explanation about raid bosses and loot drops. His words blurred into the background as Claire's gaze wandered back towards the lane.

"Sorry, I'm boring you," he said, snapping her attention back.

"No, it's not that," she replied, forcing herself to focus. "There's been an unexpected development with the new house."

"Don't tell me the dining room damp is back already. You spent a fortune having that fixed."

"Worse," she said, bracing herself. "Squatters."

Damon's eyes widened. "Like people?"

"Not *like* people," she said, sighing. "*Actual* people."

"Mate, that's mad. I should warn Sally. She was

planning to surprise you tonight with champagne to celebrate your first night."

"Well, she still can," Claire said, though the conviction in her voice wavered. "They'll be gone soon."

"Where are they going to go?"

Claire hesitated. "I don't know."

The driver dumped the last of the boxes with a pointed thud. Claire signed for them, and they carried the load into the shop, manoeuvring around the circular display piled high with spiced orange candles. She'd made more than enough this year—a lesson learned after last Christmas, when the frosted plum scent had sold out in record time. The giant plum pudding attempt at the market had helped sales soar, but the murder of the chef behind it had turned the festive commotion into something darker—and, strangely, even more profitable.

"Have you thought about asking Em?" Damon asked, unwinding his scarf as he nodded in the direction of the narrowboat Em usually kept moored behind the pub across the square. "She's always got an eye out for people. I bet she'd know somewhere."

"Em's off at some yoga retreat until the New Year. She doesn't, and I quote, 'enjoy the capitalist extremes the season pushes people to.'"

He hummed in agreement. "Sounds like Em. Well, wherever those squatters go, it's not your problem."

"And yet," Claire said, "they've made it mine."

Damon patted a box. "Want me to unpack? You haven't even taken off your coat. I can feel you itching to run off."

"Yes, please," she said. "Thanks, mate. I can't focus right now."

"No problem, boss," he said, though he lingered, rubbing the back of his neck. "Actually, I wanted to ask you something. About Sally. It's important, but—"

Claire raised an eyebrow. "But?"

"Never mind." He waved it off. "It can wait. You're in a rush."

"Good," Claire replied. "I'm not sure I can handle another surprise today."

Leaving Damon to unpack the delivery, she headed for the cul-de-sac, itching with worry about what awaited her.

* * *

Birch Close was silent. No Christmas lights twinkled in the windows, no muffled hum of televisions, nor the comforting clatter of breakfast dishes. Only the faint whistle of the wind wound through the scaffolding.

Claire hesitated at the broken gate. Something felt off.

Had they left at first light?

Somehow, the stillness didn't feel like relief. She considered circling around to check for movement at the back, but she had a key—there was no reason not to go through the front.

Squeezing through the gap in the broken gate, she walked to the door. She was worried that the squatters might have changed the locks during the night. But her key still slotted in, turning with an unsettling familiarity.

It had been months since Sally Halliwell, Damon's girlfriend, another of her oldest friends, and the estate agent who'd overseen the sale, had handed over the keys halfway through summer. They'd nearly moved in then, but the idea of living in a building site had lost its charm quickly. Fielding quotes for all the necessary work had turned into a logistical nightmare.

First, there was the damp. Then the hairline crack running along the left side of the house. And the lead flashing on the roof that needed replacing. The ridge tiles had been halfway removed and reset when the weather turned foul.

"Can't do anything until it's warmer," Tony the builder had said, rocking on his heels in that maddening way builders did. "Otherwise, frost'll get in, and it'll crumble away."

"When will it be warm enough?" Claire had asked, already dreading the answer.

Tony had sucked air through his teeth. "Weather's funny these days, isn't it? What do they call it? Global warming?" He'd rolled his eyes. "Late Feb, maybe March at the latest? You could move in and make do. Seen people live in worse. It's not pretty, but it's safe."

Safe.

The word echoed in her mind as Claire nudged the door open with her key. It swung inward, the hinges groaning despite the fresh oil she'd applied not long ago. The hollow creak reverberated through the empty house, making her wince. The door hadn't been locked. It hadn't even been fully shut.

Had they left in a hurry?

She stepped inside, holding her breath as she strained to listen for any sound—footsteps above, a door creaking, voices murmuring. Nothing.

"*Hello?*" Claire called, her voice cutting through the stillness. It echoed, a lonely sound swallowed by the bare walls and unfinished floors. "It's Claire. One of the owners."

Above her, she heard the faint creak of movement. Her breath escaped in a shaky exhale. They were still here. And now, she had to be the one to kick them out. She'd dreaded this moment since the instant her eyes had opened that morning.

"Look, I know it's not ideal," she called, gripping the paint-stripped banister for support. "But if you don't go, my boyfriend *will* call the police, and I'm not going to stop him." She paused, her gaze falling to the scuffed floorboards, guilt twisting in her chest. "I gave you the night. Now it's morning. It's time to move on."

When no one answered, Claire steeled herself and

crept further down the hallway towards the kitchen. The house felt different now. The traces of life that had clung to it yesterday—the clutter, the muffled voices—were gone, replaced by an oppressive, suffocating stillness.

She passed the sitting room, looking over the half-stripped wallpaper and the forgotten pile of old tools in the corner. Nothing stirred.

Her footsteps carried her to the kitchen, where she froze in the doorway.

Jodie lay crumpled on the dusty floorboards, her body twisted, her head bent at an unnatural angle. Blood spread beneath her in a glossy, growing pool, creeping into the gaps between the boards. The stark red was a violent contrast against the pale floorboards—boards she'd painstakingly sanded to a fresh brightness with her hands.

Pale no more.

* * *

Claire pressed her back against the cold plaster of the hallway, her breath ragged. She could taste the metallic tang of blood in her throat, even though she hadn't stepped close enough to smell it. Jodie's twisted form lingered behind her eyelids, every detail too precise.

A sound from upstairs snapped her out of her frozen state—a faint creak, barely more than a whisper. She whipped her head towards the staircase, every nerve on edge. Could someone still be here?

She forced herself to move, the old floorboards groaning under her weight. Her pulse thudded in her ears, drowning out reason. One more step, and then—

The phone rang in her hand, making her jump. Claire scrambled to answer, her voice a strained whisper.

"Ramsbottom?" she managed.

"Claire? What's wrong? The station said you'd called."

She swallowed hard, her throat dry. "There's been a murder. At my house. My *new* house. I found the body." She hesitated, glancing towards the darkened staircase. "I think someone might still be here."

A creak on the stairs sent her heart racing. Claire pressed herself against the wall, the phone trembling in her hand.

"Miss Harris?" Ramsbottom's voice crackled. "Are you safe? Lock yourself in a room if—"

"We're on our way!" a familiar voice called out from the stairs, sharp and cutting. "Just because we're homeless doesn't mean we're morning people. But we're very grateful for—"

Claire whipped around as Maria appeared, her steps measured but purposeful as she walked downstairs. The older woman stopped at the bottom, her gaze locking on the scene in the kitchen below.

The words died in Maria's throat as her eyes fell on Jodie's body, her face twisting in shock.

"*Jodie*," she gasped. She dropped to her knees beside

her, pressing her fingers to her neck. After a tense moment, she looked up, her expression a mixture of horror and anger. "What have you done?"

Claire barely registered the words.

"Maria?" came another voice, softer, hesitant. Lucy appeared in the hallway. She hovered near the wall, her frame rigid and unmoving. "*Jodie!*"

The phone in Claire's hand buzzed again. "Miss Harris? Are you still there?"

"Yes," she rasped, clutching it tighter. "I'm here."

"Officers are on their way."

Claire nodded, though her focus remained on Maria and Lucy.

"I didn't do anything," she said, her voice shaking. "I found her like this."

Lucy didn't move, her expression as blank as fresh snow, her eyes stuck on Jodie's broken form as though she were staring at nothing at all.

Claire shivered. That stare chilled her more than the winter frost outside ever could.

* * *

Birch Close was still eerily quiet when the police arrived. Their cars rolled into the cul-de-sac, blue lights cutting through the hazy morning sky. The usual crowd of curtain-twitchers had yet to emerge—it was too early and far too cold, even for them.

Claire's breath hung in the frosty air as she made her

way around to the back garden. She found Maria and Lucy leaning against the back of the house.

"I need to ask you both something," Claire began, her voice low so as not to draw attention from the officers bustling inside.

Maria's expression hardened. "We don't have to talk to you."

Claire ignored the jab. "Did you hear or see anything last night? Anything unusual?"

"We slept through the night," Maria replied instantly. "Didn't hear a thing. Did we, Lucy?"

Lucy glanced at Maria, her lip caught between her teeth, before nodding. "Nothing."

The way Maria's hand rested on Lucy's shoulder made Claire uneasy. The younger woman looked like she wanted to say more but didn't dare.

"Lucy?" Claire pressed, trying to meet her gaze.

"She said we didn't hear anything," Maria snapped, her voice sharp as a knife. Her grip on Lucy's shoulder tightened. "We don't know anything. What's more, I reckon *you're* the one with questions to answer."

"What's that supposed to mean?" Claire asked, startled.

"It makes sense, doesn't it?" Maria said with a dead-eyed stare. "*You* wanted us gone. *You* found her. You've practically got blood on your hands."

Claire's jaw tightened. "I didn't."

"Yeah," Maria retorted. "Neither did we."

Claire opened her mouth to reply, but Lucy's downcast eyes and the rigid line of Maria's shoulders stopped her. She wasn't going to get anywhere with them, not now.

Detective Inspector Harry Ramsbottom's voice carried on the wind, and Claire turned and hurried back to the front as DI Ramsbottom lumbered out of his tiny car. He clung to his defiant golden toupee as it fluttered in the wind, the other clutching a battered notebook. Despite his mismatched appearance and slow, deliberate gait, his presence commanded attention, though not for the right reasons.

"Terrible, terrible business," he announced, addressing Claire, his eyes on her parents' house. "I don't suppose your father is up and about yet? Alan's bound to be cooking up theories already."

"I haven't woken them," she replied, her voice small. She cleared her throat, but the lump wouldn't budge. "I don't think she's been dead long. The blood was still pooling when I found her."

"Kitchen, you said?" Inside the house, Ramsbottom's voice rang with calm authority. "Let's get started, folks!"

Officers filed in with quiet precision, unpacking cases and setting up equipment. The sterile sounds of snapping gloves and the faint hum of machinery filled the air.

Claire hovered near the front doorway, and she

couldn't seem to move as Ramsbottom knelt beside Jodie's body.

"What have we got?" he asked.

The forensic officer didn't look up as they replied, "Female, mid-to-late-thirties. Blunt force trauma to the back of the head. Body's still slightly warm. Time of death—roughly an hour ago."

Claire's stomach churned at the clinical delivery but forced herself to listen. She'd been right—Jodie hadn't been dead long.

"Hmm." Ramsbottom pushed himself to his feet with a grunt, brushing dust off his trousers. "Start combing the scene. I want everything catalogued."

As the forensic team began their work, Claire stood frozen, watching as fragments of the truth began to emerge.

One officer rummaged through the bin and pulled out a charred scrap of paper. Slipping it into a plastic evidence bag, they handed it to Ramsbottom. He squinted at the faint markings on the singed edges.

"*C.H., L.R., R.G.,*" he read aloud, his brow furrowing. "What do we reckon—initials or a code?"

"Fresh paint on her jacket," another officer noted, snapping photos. "Could be significant."

"Good eye," Ramsbottom said, nodding before turning to another officer, who was bagging something they'd pulled from Jodie's fingers.

"Fishing wire?" Ramsbottom suggested, holding up the evidence bag. The frayed ends glinted under the light. "Or invisible string?"

"A guitar string?" Claire suggested before she had time to think. "There was a guitar here."

"Search the place for a guitar," he ordered. "Good spot, Claire. This does look like a guitar string."

His attention, however, shifted to the stainless-steel sink beneath the window—the one part of the kitchen that hadn't been ripped out during renovations. An officer pulled out a hammer from the basin. It gleamed unnaturally clean, the polished metal catching the light.

Standing on the doorstep, Claire realised how much she'd missed earlier in her shock: the burnt note, the guitar string, the paint streaks. She'd only seen the body.

"No blood," Ramsbottom observed, holding up the hammer. "Odd, considering the mess."

"It *is* in a sink, sir," the forensic officer pointed out. "Could have been washed?"

"Is this tap working?" Ramsbottom called towards Claire.

"I don't know."

"Yes," Maria interjected from behind, her voice steady. "It's one of the reasons we picked this place. It's cold, but it's on." Under her breath, she added, "That and the unlocked back door."

The sound of scuffling came from above before two

officers dragged Stuart down the stairs. His face was flushed, his bloodshot eyes squinting against the light, and he stumbled as they pulled him upright.

"Drank himself to sleep," Maria muttered, crossing her arms as she stood in the overgrown garden beside Lucy, who remained silent, her wide eyes fixed on the kitchen doorway. "Again."

Stuart's gaze landed on the hammer being bagged. "That's mine!"

"I should have known," Ramsbottom stated sharply. "Stuart Shipton, correct? We've met before. I arrested you six months ago."

"And for what?" Stuart scowled, his lips curling in defiance. "Taking what was mine after they owed me wages?"

"Ah, yes," Ramsbottom replied, his tone laced with dry amusement. "That's what you said then. You destroyed thousands of pounds worth of machinery on your old building site during your rampage and stole five hundred pounds in cash from the office."

"And I was still owed double that! It's your fault I can't get a job on any site. My name's been dragged through the mud."

Ramsbottom raised the bagged hammer. "And this? Your hammer, found at the scene?"

"What scene?" Stuart muttered, jerking away from the officers to step fully into the hall. His eyes locked on

Jodie's lifeless form. Like Lucy, he didn't offer much of a reaction. "I didn't do anything."

"You expect me to believe that?"

"Check the hammer!" Stuart's composure cracked, his voice rising. "You think I'd kill her when I was trying to get my money back? Use your head! I gave her that five hundred quid because she promised to double it."

Claire couldn't stay silent. "How?" she asked, stepping over the threshold.

"None of *your* business." His tone was sharp. "Unless I'm under arrest, I'm not sticking around."

"You're not under arrest." Ramsbottom raised a hand, calm but firm. "*Yet*. But don't think for a second you're free to leave. You so much as step outside Northash, and I'll have you arrested faster than you can say 'hammer time.'"

Stuart scowled but said nothing.

"Where are my boots?" he cried. "I left them here by the door."

"I haven't seen any," Claire replied.

"Bloody typical!"

Stuart stormed off, and out in the garden, Maria stood with her arms crossed, her face tight. She watched Stuart go, shaking her head, as though him storming off were a familiar scene.

Claire hoped for answers from Maria, who'd been the most level of the group, but the older woman wouldn't meet her eyes. Her hands fidgeted with the hem of her jumper, her knuckles pale. Beside her, Lucy remained motionless, her expression unreadable. Without a word, she slipped around the gate and disappeared in the opposite direction. Maria hesitated, then followed.

Claire watched them disappear towards the village, a question lingering in her mind: would she ever see them again?

As her gaze shifted, she noticed someone else near the old street sign, just beyond the garden fence. A figure lingered in the fog. A man. She pushed her glasses up, narrowing her eyes. She recognised him—last night's runner. Ricky with the shaggy hair. The man who had burst out of the house twice, fleeing as though escaping a fight.

Lucy had called him their leader—the one who kept them safe.

"Ricky?" Claire called out.

But before she could get close, the rumble of an engine shattered the stillness. Janet's Angels cleaning van trundled up the lane, its halo-and-wings logo—more suited to a funeral home than a cleaning company—gleaming faintly through the fog.

Claire glanced back at the street sign. Ricky was gone, swallowed by the rolling fog from the countryside.

"What on earth?" Janet called as the van slowed to a stop beside Claire. She leaned out of the driver's window, squinting at the police tape being crisscrossed over the front door. "All this for *squatters*?"

Claire let out a slow breath. "All this for murder, Mother."

"*Murder?*" Her eyes widened as she ducked to shake her head at Claire. "Oh, love, what have you got tangled up in now?"

Following the van to her parents' house, Claire glimpsed through the sitting room window. Inside, Ryan and the kids were having breakfast in front of the TV. Hugo played on his console between bites while Amelia reached for another slice of toast slathered in chocolate spread. It looked so ordinary. Warm. Untouched by the storm brewing outside.

Murder. Secrets. Unanswered questions. They swirled in her mind, relentless as the light snow drifting through the thick fog. Something bigger was closing in around her—vast, inescapable, pulling her deeper into its grip.

So much for one more day.

CHAPTER FIVE

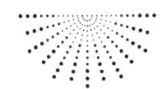

In her father's shed at the bottom of the garden, Claire perched on her usual upturned terracotta plant pot in the corner, its ridges pressing into her thighs. The earthy scent of soil and rust filled the small space as her father oiled a pair of shears at his old potting desk.

She cradled a mug of coffee in her palms, wincing at the bitter taste. She'd been so distracted earlier she couldn't remember how many scoops she'd added.

"I went back to the house last night," she began.

Alan didn't look up, but his hands paused for a fraction of a second before resuming their rhythm.

"They were all inside—acting like it was theirs." Claire exhaled, the words tumbling out in a disjointed rush. "The one I told you ran away? Ricky. He'd come back for his guitar. He was sitting on the sofa, playing some miserable chords. Lucy was in the corner with a sketchbook, just scribbling. Maria was darning socks." She paused, gripping the mug tighter. "And Jodie was standing by the fireplace, giving orders like she was running the place. Stuart was carving into the kitchen table—*my* table. It was so surreal."

Alan gave a slight nod but didn't interrupt.

"And Lucy," Claire continued, her voice faltering. "I found her in the garden later, crying. She kept muttering that she hated someone. *I hate her.* In a loop, and she looked so broken."

"You think she was talking about Jodie?" Alan suggested.

"Maybe, but when I tried to talk to her, Jodie barked at Lucy to get inside, and she just obeyed. Like she didn't have a choice."

"I noticed last night that Maria also has a hold over that girl," Alan admitted, still not looking up. "And it sounds like Jodie's no better. Alibis?"

"I tried to ask, but Maria wasn't in a chatty mood." She laughed at the understatement, sipping her coffee. "But you're right—she wouldn't let Lucy talk, and I was sure Lucy wanted to say something."

"She's young," he said. "Easily swayed. And Maria doesn't trust easily, that much is clear. You noticed how she clammed up when she recognised me from my old life. To her, you're the daughter of the police. As good as, in her eyes."

"There's more." Claire rubbed at her temples. "I saw Carol and Kris fighting next door. I mean *really* fighting. I couldn't figure out what it was about, but Carol threw a poinsettia at the wall. Kris laughed and walked away like it wasn't the first time."

Alan sighed, his expression darkening. "I don't like to gossip about my neighbours, but there's been more noise coming from Carol and Kris' side lately. I've suspected they've been heading for divorce for a while. I keep thinking I should talk to them."

"You know how Carol would react."

"Hmm," he agreed. "Right you are, little one."

"And I tried to help Ricky," she continued, the words tumbling out. "Offered him this shed for the night. Told him there's a heater in here." She shook her head. "He just screamed out in the night, then left. Walked down to the village. I didn't know what else to do."

Alan reached over, his hand resting on her knee. "You did what you could."

"It doesn't feel like enough." Claire swallowed hard, blinking against the stinging in her eyes. "I really hated Jodie, and I'd only known her a day, but—"

"Now imagine how much the others despised her," Alan assured her, ducking to meet her eyes. "Nobody deserves to meet an end like that, but from where I'm sitting, Jodie wasn't a savoury character, and you've outlined the most likely suspects for her demise."

For a moment, the shed was silent save for the faint rustle of the wind outside. Claire cleared her throat, forcing herself to continue.

"You know," Claire began again, "you were right last night. If we'd called Ramsbottom, they might have scattered before they made it into the cells. Before a woman had to die. She wasn't nice, but she was alive."

Alan leaned against the workbench, abandoning the sheers. His steady presence had always been a balm for Claire's nerves.

"This isn't your fault, little one," he said. "This is bad luck. That house next door, on the other side—it's been empty for years. They could've easily picked that one."

Claire's fingers laced together around her mug. "But that one didn't have a back door unlocked." Her voice wavered. "I think that was *me*, Dad. I was the last one in there. I don't remember locking it."

He smiled kindly. "No, we don't tend to remember the things we don't do. But it's still not your fault."

"Maria thought so," Claire muttered, her knuckles whitening around the mug. "She jumped straight to that conclusion. How long before Carol and Kris think the same—and it spreads around the cul-de-sac?"

"Since when have you cared what everyone thinks of you?" Alan asked, raising a brow. "Chin up. You're a

Harris. We're made of tough stuff. Ramsbottom will get to the bottom of this."

"I can't just stand by," Claire said, her voice trembling. "I promised Hugo we'd be in that house. I promised myself." She exhaled slowly, steadying herself. "There was so much left at the crime scene. A hammer that belongs to Stuart."

Alan's brow furrowed. "The fella who said Jodie owed him money?"

She nodded. "He brought it up again. Jodie offered to double it."

"Hmm. What else?"

"A broken guitar string," she added, glancing down at her hands. "It was wrapped around her fingers. And there was a scrap of paper with initials… C something. I can't remember the rest. I should've taken notes—"

The shed door creaked open, cutting him off. Janet stepped inside, her expression one of sheer distaste as she surveyed the cluttered space. She pinched her nose as though the air might poison her and hopped over a stray pair of boots, her movements as careful as if she were navigating a minefield.

"*Guess* what I saw this morning!" she announced as if she'd wandered into a garden party rather than a grimy shed.

"A dirty office you couldn't wait to clean, my love?" Alan replied.

"Several," Janet admitted with a sniff. "But something far more shocking than that. Go on, Claire."

"Mother," Claire said flatly, "how could I possibly guess?"

"Fine!" Janet huffed. "I saw our *lovely* neighbour, Carol Hodgkinson, talking to one of those squatters across the garden fence."

Claire sat upright. "Which one?"

"I'm not sure," Janet said, waving a dismissive hand. "They were all bundled up in layers hours before sunrise. Carol's never usually up. Had her rollers in—she's always sworn her bouncy curls were natural. Glad I'm not running around in her Women's Institute circles anymore. Did you know she claimed the lead in the choir but refused to audition? The *nerve!*"

"As riveting as that is," Claire interrupted, "what were they doing?"

"I *told* you. Talking over the fence."

Alan rubbed his temples. "About what, dear?"

"My hearing is good, but not that good!" Janet sighed. "They were whispering. Arguing, it looked like."

"Carol isn't one to keep her voice down," Claire pointed out.

"She must have known them," Alan stated with a sure nod. "Ramsbottom should hear about it."

"I already told him," Janet replied, lifting her chin. "He's in our sitting room getting crumbs all over the carpet and ploughing through those M&S mince pies I bought. Alan, I think he wants to talk to you."

Janet turned and marched back towards the house. Claire and Alan exchanged glances before following.

IN THE SITTING ROOM, RAMSBOTTOM SAT ON THE SOFA with a half-eaten mince pie. The plate on the coffee table was nearly empty, and his teacup sat steaming beside it. Janet bustled around him, mini vacuum in hand.

"Delicious," Ramsbottom remarked, licking a crumb from his thumb. "So buttery and light. Did you make these yourself?"

"Of course," Janet lied smoothly. "What did *she* have to say for herself?"

"I spoke to Carol and Kris." Ramsbottom leaned back, flipping through his notebook. "They both claim they were in bed, fast asleep all morning, and only awoke when they heard all the police cars pull up. Carol says *you're* lying, Janet."

"I would never!" Janet gasped as she shifted the M&S box under a stack of magazines before topping up his tea from the pot. "*She's* the liar. I saw her as clear as day!"

"You said it was still dark," he reminded her, flicking back a page and sending more crumbs onto the carpet.

"It *was* dark," Janet shot back before firing off another

blast of the vacuum. "But I *saw* her. I've never liked that woman."

Janet hurried out of the room, and Claire's attention shifted to the staircase, where Ryan stood with Amelia and Hugo. The kids hovered just behind him, peeking cautiously around the banister.

Leaving her father to talk shop with his former colleague—once a man who had worked under him—Claire slipped into the hall.

"What's going on?" Amelia asked.

"There's been an incident at the new house," she said. "A woman has died."

"Died?" Amelia replied, eyes widening slightly. "Maybe her ghost will haunt the place. Can we go and see?"

Ryan ushered them back upstairs. "Go get dressed. You've got your art club in an hour."

Amelia trudged upstairs, muttering something about already being dressed, but Hugo lingered, his small hand gripping the banister. He looked up at Claire, his face unusually serious, his brows drawn together in quiet thought.

"Were you scared?" Hugo asked after a pause.

Claire swallowed hard, nodding. "I was," she admitted. "But I'm okay now. We're all okay."

Hugo hesitated, then leaned in and gave her a quick hug. Claire's arms closed around him, and she held him tightly, resisting the sting of tears pricking her eyes. The hug was brief, but it stayed with her as she watched him scurry upstairs after his sister.

Ryan stepped closer, his hands sliding over her shoulders. Without a word, he pulled her into a hug—stronger and tighter than Hugo's. Claire let herself sink into it, feeling the tension in her chest ease, if only slightly.

"I was supposed to come with you," he said.

"I remembered a delivery for the shop and—" She rested her forehead against his chest. "I'm sorry."

Ryan pulled back just enough to meet her eyes. "Why are you sorry?"

"Because…" Her voice wavered as she searched for the words. "… I could have stopped this."

"You were being decent last night."

"And someone took advantage of that."

"You wouldn't have done it any differently, Claire." Ryan cupped her face, his expression softening. "That's who you are."

"And now someone's dead," she whispered. "One of those squatters killed him, Ryan. They had to have." She sighed, wishing she could turn back the clock. "I *need* to know why."

CHAPTER SIX

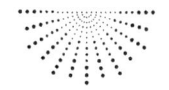

*L*ater that morning, as Claire walked through the cul-de-sac on her way back to work, something moved out of the corner of her eye. Carol Hodgkinson was crouched near the fence, her gloved hands poised over a small, soggy pile of frostbitten leaves.

"Carol?" Claire called, trying not to sound accusatory.

Carol straightened with a jerk like she'd been caught doing something unspeakable.

"*What?*" she cried.

Claire raised an eyebrow. "What are you doing?"

"Someone's got to keep the place tidy, and clearly, that someone *isn't* you."

Claire folded her arms. "Dead leaves?"

"Yes, dead leaves," Carol said firmly, scooping up a few

and tossing them into a plastic carrier bag. "Do you think they'll move themselves? This house might be yours, but it's still part of the neighbourhood. A little upkeep wouldn't hurt."

Claire took a step closer, her gaze narrowing. "You're out here in the cold, cleaning up dead leaves when the police are in there combing over a crime scene?"

Carol huffed. "I'm retired, Claire. I've got time on my hands, unlike you. Haven't you got a shop to go and run?"

"Do I?" Claire replied, arching a brow. "Thank you for your concern. But you don't have to keep up my garden for me."

Carol sniffed, tossing the bag over her shoulder. "Then get on top of it."

"Last night," Claire called after her, her voice cutting through the crisp morning air. "Is everything alright?"

Carol froze mid-step. Her shoulders tensed as she turned back to Claire. Her face was a battlefield of emotions—anger, embarrassment, and something Claire couldn't quite name—flashing across her features like fireworks–she knew what Claire was hinting at.

"Mind your own business," Carol growled, her voice low and sharp.

"Likewise."

Claire took the bag from Carol and tipped the contents back onto her garden, dead leaves scattering across the frosty ground. With deliberate precision, she folded the now-empty bag and handed it back to Carol.

"If you'd caught me in your garden like that," Claire said, "I'm sure you'd have accused me of trespassing."

Carol's jaw tightened, her nostrils flaring. Without another word, she spun on her heel and stormed back to her house, the door slamming shut behind her with a resounding crack.

For a moment, Claire stared at the closed door. Her gut twisted. Carol had been lying—Claire was sure of it. But if she wasn't here for the dead leaves, then what had she been looking for?

Crouching where Carol had been rummaging, Claire brushed aside the scattered leaves with her fingertips. She sifted through the frozen undergrowth, searching for what? She didn't know.

After a few fruitless minutes, she sat back on her heels and sighed. Maybe Carol had already found whatever she'd been looking for. Or perhaps it had been about the leaves.

"*Neighbours,*" Claire muttered, setting off again.

The shop was unusually quiet for noon on Saturday in December, the kind of lull Claire usually welcomed. Normally, she'd use the time to jot down new scent formulas in her little black book or dust the backs of the shelves. Today, she didn't want to do either.

With Damon napping in the worn leather chair in the stockroom, she was left alone with her thoughts—and their relentless chatter was starting to wear thin.

The door jingled, breaking the silence, as Eugene Cropper swept in. Snow dusted his lion's mane of a beard.

"Claire!" he bellowed, stomping snow off his boots. "I need your finest Christmas candles."

Claire forced a smile, moving to the display tables. "You're in luck. We've just restocked."

"Smells divine in here, as always." Eugene leaned in, squinting at the labels. "What do you recommend for someone who's got everything but manners?"

"My new spiced orange is my current favourite."

"Then I'll take two!" he said as she wrapped the candles. "Guess who I got for Secret Santa in the choir this year?"

Claire raised an eyebrow. "Camila Parker Bowles?"

"Oh, you are wicked!" Eugene chuckled, his frilly cravat shaking under his beard—he was easily Northash's most eccentric dresser. "*Worse*. Carol Hodgkinson. Isn't she your mother's neighbour?"

"And mine," Claire said before adding, "if I ever get to move in."

"I hate to speak ill of your neighbours, but she's

delightfully *awful*. Always nagging about tempo or hogging the front row like she's auditioning for the West End, yet she can't sing a note in tune. I tried to switch, but nobody wanted her. Even Marjorie, and she'd take a puppy with fleas."

Claire chuckled. "Sounds like Carol."

"A battle-axe!" Eugene said without hesitation. "She has a sharp tongue and sharper elbows than sense!"

"Violent?" Claire asked, her curiosity piqued.

"Oh, I wouldn't go *that* far," he said, though he hesitated. "Although, she did almost run over Marley last week. She was reversing quite fast, and Marley's rather slim. She said she didn't see him, but then blamed him anyway. I think she was jealous that my Marley has the voice of an angel and she sings like an old goose that is really perturbed about being a goose."

Claire fought a laugh, biting her lip as she slid the wrapped candles across the counter. Eugene straightened, brushing the snow from his sleeves.

"What's this I hear about *murder* in your new house? Ramsbottom was in the café earlier, looking as confused as ever as he ate us out of house and home."

Claire stiffened. "Trouble with some squatters. One of them turned up dead."

Eugene's brows shot up. "Well, If anyone can sort it, it's you. You've got the grit of a good terrier. Never let go once you've sunk your teeth in."

"Thanks, Eugene," Claire said. "I'll take that as a compliment?"

"Good! Because I meant it as one." He tipped an imaginary hat and turned towards the door. "Good luck with Carol, by the way. She's bound to get in your way."

"She already has," Claire muttered as the door jingled shut behind him.

LATER THAT AFTERNOON, AS CLAIRE WORKED THROUGH THE growing rush in the shop, she kept returning to thoughts of Carol. She inhaled the latest Star Candle of the Month as she bagged up three for one lady, the faint scent of spiced orange rising to meet her. It was her current favourite, but the warmth it usually brought her didn't settle her.

Carol's deflection, her reputation, even her supposed 'accident' with Marley—it didn't sit right. Claire had spent enough time around difficult people to know that sharp tongues were often shields. But what was Carol hiding behind hers? Could someone like her really have crossed the line into murder? She'd thrown that plant without a second thought.

A shout from the counter pulled Claire from her thoughts, where Damon was attempting to appease a customer with his usual awkward charm. Whatever the truth about Carol was, she'd find it—just not right now.

For now, she had the shop to survive. The festive playlist hummed in the background, and she caught Damon's eye. His shrug told her all she needed to know: Christmas madness had officially arrived. She grabbed another box of candles from the back, letting herself focus on the day ahead. There'd be time to dig deeper later.

But as she restocked, a tap on her shoulder made her jump. "Excuse me, but this candle doesn't smell of *anything*," a customer said, holding up a jar with a frown.

Claire plastered on her brightest *of course you're right, you're the customer* smile and gave the candle a sniff. It smelled exactly like the others—sweet vanilla musk, strong and unmistakable. Another victim of 'shop nose.' The woman had numbed her sense of smell by testing every candle on display, and she was the fourth person today with the same complaint.

Claire reached for another candle, but her hand trembled.

"How about this one?" she asked.

The woman inhaled deeply. "Nope."

"You don't smell black cherry?"

"Nope."

Claire grabbed another. "Toffee apple?"

"Nothing."

She tried again, holding up a third jar. "Candy cane?"

"No." The woman huffed, her frustration growing. "I heard these were the best candles around. I travelled twenty minutes, and my mother is very particular, and *all* she wanted for Christmas was a—"

Claire set the candle down, her forced smile faltering. Despite everything she knew about running her shop, she fled, leaving the woman mid-sentence.

She darted around the counter and slipped into the storeroom. Leaning against the island, cluttered with spring scent samples—lemon, jasmine, peach—she tried to slow her breathing. Her eyes closed, but instead of calm, she saw blood spreading across freshly sanded floorboards.

How could she ever look at that house the same way again?

"Did you eat breakfast?" Damon's voice cut through her spiralling thoughts as he popped his head into the storeroom.

"How could I?" She ran a hand through her fine hair, sticking to her scalp. She sighed, frustration spilling over. She couldn't remember the last time she'd eaten—or had a moment to breathe.

"Get us some lunch." Damon snapped open the till, pulled out a purple twenty-pound note, and shoved it into her hand. "You're a liability right now, and you're not yourself when you're hungry."

Claire blinked, half ready to argue, but her empty stomach twisted in agreement. She didn't want to leave Damon to face the crowd alone, but staying would only make things worse. With a reluctant sigh, she grabbed her coat and hat.

"Fine," she agreed, pulling them on. "But I'll be quick."

Outside, she zipped her coat against the chill and threaded her way through the bustling Christmas market. The noise and smells swirled around her—roasting chestnuts, spiced cider, freshly baked bread. She took in the stalls, half expecting to catch a glimpse of one of the squatters.

DI Ramsbottom had been by earlier, his tone as casually dismissive as ever.

"Any idea where they're staying now?" he'd asked.

"They don't live *anywhere*," she'd replied.

"Good point. You know, it could've been random. Someone sneaking in, looking for a place to kip, and finding Jodie instead?"

"At six in the morning?"

"It *has* been cold."

She'd stopped herself from answering. Was he trying to say there was no solving this case despite the pile of evidence around Jodie's body? Now, weaving through the crowd, that same concern crept in. The squatters could be anywhere.

Claire's gaze landed on Carol and Kris at an ornament stall, their voices cutting through the market's hum.

"You *cannot* put silver with gold," Kris said, exasperated. "It clashes."

"No, it doesn't!" Carol snapped, holding up a glittering gold star. "You don't know anything about interior design. You never compromise."

"Do things *your* way, you mean? I don't like silver and gold together. Pick one."

Claire stared in disbelief. How could they argue about colour schemes so casually after what had happened next door? Then Carol caught her watching. Her hand jerked, and the star slipped, shattering on the cobblestones.

"Happy now?" Carol shouted, her voice rising.

Kris waved her off with a dismissive hand and stormed towards The Hesketh Arms. Carol, fuming, stomped in the opposite direction.

"You need to pay for that!" the stallholder called after them, but neither looked back.

"Sorry about her." Claire stepped closer, wincing. "She's my neighbour. I can pay for this."

The stallholder shook her head and crouched to gather the shards. "It's fine," she muttered. "There are worse things going on. Hear about that dead woman?"

"I did," she said carefully, sensing an opportunity. "Did you catch what they were arguing about?"

"Something about her not being where *she* said *she* was. That's how he put it, anyway. He didn't look happy."

Claire scanned the market for Carol, but she was gone. Was Kris hinting at their alibi being a lie? Carol had claimed they'd been in bed all morning, but her mother had spotted Carol out earlier. Janet's brutal honesty might be a blessing for once.

She thanked the stallholder and bought a small ornament—a hand-painted robin perched on a branch. She tucked it into her pocket and headed for Marley's Café on the corner. Like her shop, it buzzed with the pre-Christmas rush.

Inside, Claire stopped short. Lucy and Maria sat at a table in the middle of the busy café, their heads close over steaming cups of tea. The sight of them, so calm after the morning, froze Claire in place.

She tugged her hat lower and hesitated before joining the back of the queue. Had they noticed her? Lucy's gaze flicked her way but didn't linger, offering no sign of recognition.

Claire kept them in her peripheral vision, the low murmur of their conversation drifting her way.

"What *projects*?" Maria asked, her voice just loud enough to carry. "You can be honest with me, Lucy."

"Just projects," Lucy replied, her tone shrinking. "I don't want to talk about it."

"And you don't have to," Maria said, soft but firm. "But

you need to get your story straight. They're going to link Jodie back to you sooner or later. We both know she was dodgy."

"She was looking after us," Lucy whispered.

"Was she?" Maria snorted. "You saw how she treated Ricky last night. The second Ricky questioned our long-term plans, Jodie flipped out."

"She doesn't like talking about the future."

"*Didn't*," Maria corrected, letting the word hang in the air. "Jodie must've known this was coming. She crossed everyone, Lucy, and she didn't care whose toes she stepped on. Kicking Ricky out like that, knowing how you feel about him—"

"*Felt*," Lucy interrupted sharply.

"If you say so." Maria sighed, a long, drawn-out exhale. "Any one of us could've been next. You know Jodie had dirt on everyone and wasn't afraid to use it. I hate to say it, but she wasn't a good person."

"I know, but she was my sister."

Claire's stomach churned. Jodie was Lucy's sister? Did that explain the blank expression, the eerie detachment? She couldn't imagine Amelia or Hugo reacting so stoically if something happened to one of them.

Before she could process the revelation further, someone tapped her shoulder. Claire spun, half-expecting to be caught eavesdropping, but it was Sally Halliwell.

"Oh, mate," Sally said, pulling her into a hug. "I'm so sorry all this is happening. You've waited so long, and now…"

"It's fine," Claire replied, though the waver in her voice betrayed her. "Actually, it's not."

Sally sighed. "These things happen. Empty houses attract trouble. People break in and do all sorts of damage. I heard the back door was unlocked?"

Claire glanced at Maria and Lucy's table, but it had been claimed by a woman with a pram. Their cups were still steaming on the table, but they'd slipped out quietly, unnoticed. Again.

"They were just trying to stay warm," Claire said as the queue shuffled forward. "I gave them the night, and to their credit, some of them were leaving."

"Leaving behind a dead woman!" Sally said, biting her lip as though holding back more. She leaned closer. "I know it's off-topic, but has Damon been acting strange to you?"

Claire raised an eyebrow, her mind flicking to his cryptic comment early that morning about needing to discuss something 'important.' The shop had been too busy for her to follow up, but Sally didn't need to know that.

"Damon's always strange," she said lightly. "It's why we love him."

"Stranger than usual," Sally pressed, fidgeting. "I don't

know. He just seems off. He wouldn't break up with me before Christmas, would he?"

"C'mon, Sally. No."

"You're right," she said, shaking her head, though her doubt lingered. "I'm being silly."

"He adores you," Claire said. "Really."

Sally smiled, but uncertainty flashed in her eyes. Still, she didn't push the topic further.

"So, what's the plan with the house? The squatters will have scattered, and the police will clear everything out soon, right?"

Claire didn't answer. Her thoughts were stuck on Maria and Lucy's conversation—'projects' and 'dirt.' The queue shuffled forward.

"You know," Sally said, trying to shift the conversation, "this reminds me of when you found that body in the attic above your shop. I'm starting to think you're an estate agent's worst nightmare. Ever thought about retraining as a sniffer dog for the police?"

Claire laughed—a welcome break. But Sally's usual mischievous glint faded, replaced by something more uncertain. She bit her lip again, clearly wrestling with her thoughts.

"I can talk to Damon?" Claire offered.

"Yes… *no*… I don't know…" She tucked her caramel-coloured hair behind her ears and groaned. "I just don't want to lose him. My girls love him. *I* love him. And compared to my ex, Damon is a saint. A few years ago, I'd never have pictured myself with a nerd like him, but now?" She sighed deeply. "Oh, Claire, I hate this. I can't imagine my life without him."

Through the café window, Claire spotted Ryan trudging past, his shoulders hunched against the cold in nothing more than a vest. Her lips curved into a soft smile.

"I know the feeling," she said, patting Sally's arm. "Hold my spot. I'll be right back."

Sally nodded, her expression still clouded as Claire slipped out of the café. She'd talk to Damon when the Christmas shoppers finally thinned out, but she knew from the years of running the shop that on the penultimate Saturday before Christmas, that could take hours.

She jogged through the slushy snow to catch up with Ryan, who was heading back towards the gym from the gallery's direction. She reached him at the edge of the market.

"Hey," she called, matching his stride. "Did you accept the job?"

"Not yet," he said with a tight smile. "I popped by on my lunch break to ask about Lucy. For you."

"And they say romance is dead," Claire teased, winking. "What did you find out?"

"She was fired for *forging* paintings," Ryan said,

rubbing his arms against the cold. "Mike—the owner—didn't want to give more details. I don't think he even told the police, but he didn't want her around after that." He paused and added, "He offered me the job again."

"What did you say?"

"I told him I'd think about it," he replied, groaning. "I don't know what to do. Why did Em have to go on holiday now? She'd know exactly what to say."

Claire laughed, imagining Northash's free-spirited yoga teacher. She missed her too—she gave the best hugs.

"If Em had a mobile phone instead of relying on phone boxes," Claire said, "I'd suggest you call her, but she'd probably say something like, 'If you don't know what to do, do nothing.' But I think *you* already know the answer."

Ryan sighed, checking his watch. "I'm already over my lunch break. I can't lose the job I have while worrying about one I don't have. Can we finish this later at home?"

"Where is home right now?" she asked, half-joking.

"Wherever we are," he said, leaning in to kiss her. "With any luck, Ramsbottom's arresting someone right now."

"*If* he can find them," Claire muttered as Ryan darted behind a mulled wine stall.

Stepping back into the café, the scent of freshly baked scones and coffee teased her senses, and for the first time all day, her stomach growled—a loud reminder that Damon had been right. She wasn't herself when she was hungry.

The queue had cleared, leaving her next in line. Sally was gone, but Eugene's booming voice greeted her before she could even speak.

"Ah, Claire! Twice in one day!" he declared, beaming through his lion's mane. Wiping his hands on a tea towel, he leaned closer. "Now, while I've got you—any thoughts on joining the bowls club? After your *legendary* winning throw in Peridale this summer, we'd be honoured…"

But Claire's focus drifted, Eugene's words fading into the background. The revelation about Lucy's art forgeries —whatever form they took—swirled in her mind. Were these the 'projects' she'd been so reluctant to discuss with Maria? And the revelation that Lucy and Jodie were siblings had caught Claire off guard, given Lucy's reaction to seeing his body.

The threads were tangled, fraying at the edges yet tightening into something she couldn't quite grasp.

Whatever this was, Jodie's death wasn't a random act of violence like Ramsbottom had suggested—it had to be part of something bigger.

Damon barely mumbled a goodbye before bolting from the shop. Normally, after a busy Saturday like the one they'd had, he'd suggest they saunter across to The Hesketh Arms for a pint of homebrew and their annual 'Mystery Crispmas' flavour guessing game. This year's crisps had been a unanimous 'stuffing and nothing else,' but tonight, the usual banter was missing. Damon had practically fled.

Claire didn't have time to dwell on her friend's strange behaviour. Ryan was working late at the gym, and her mother's van idled under a street light as the Christmas market wound down for the night. Janet's beaming smile greeted her before Claire even reached the kerb.

"*Great* news!" Janet called.

"They've found Jodie's murderer?"

"*Less* great news," Janet replied, spinning a set of keys on her finger. "Ramsbottom's closed the crime scene and passed me these. Do you know what that means? We can clean up your new home!"

Claire blinked. "Right."

"Well, I was expecting a *little* more enthusiasm, dear. Aren't you pleased?"

"It's just quick, that's all."

"Quick?" Janet huffed, reaching across to toss open the passenger door. "There were daffodils blooming when your offer was accepted. It's about time you and Ryan get your happily-ever-after in that house."

Before Claire could protest, Janet ushered her into the van. They wound along the lane towards the cul-de-sac, the square shrinking in the rearview mirror as the countryside closed in around them. Crossing the canal bridge, the stillness of the night swallowed them up. It should have been calming, but for Claire, the quiet made her thoughts uncomfortably loud again.

"I think you were right about seeing Carol early this morning," Claire said, watching the streetlamps blur past, growing fewer and farther apart. "I saw her rummaging around in my dead leaves this morning. If only you saw who she was talking to."

"I *know* I was right," Janet replied firmly. "I wasn't hallucinating, dear."

Claire hesitated. "I heard something else today. Kris didn't sound too happy about Carol claiming to be somewhere she wasn't."

"Like in bed with him?" Janet sniffed. "He's always been a heavy sleeper. You can hear him snoring from the next garden over. But her? Devious witch, always flitting around. She could have easily snuck out."

"You really don't like her," Claire observed.

"Do you?"

Claire didn't need to think about it.

"No," she said.

"She's always trying to compete with me," Janet grumbled. "We get a new car, she gets a new car. We get a new kitchen, she gets a new kitchen. We plant rose bushes, she gets a hanging basket. It's *exhausting*." She sighed, as if Carol had been the bane of her existence for years. "Speaking of kitchens, I saw the most delightful country style—"

"Another time, Mum."

Grumbling about 'sales that won't last forever,' Janet pulled into the cul-de-sac. The police were gone, and the house stood silent against the darkness of the surrounding farmland.

Janet cut the engine with a huff. "I don't know about you," she started, "but I can easily picture Carol Hodgkinson clobbering a man over the head with a blunt object. Your father told me about the plant."

"Like a hammer?" Claire asked as they climbed out.

The van doors slammed, the sound echoing through the stillness. Curtains twitched at the Hodgkinson house, and Janet responded with an exaggerated wave before thrusting a basket of cleaning supplies into Claire's arms. From the van's back, she dragged out her trusty Henry Hoover.

"It wasn't a hammer," Janet said in a matter-of-fact tone. "Not the one they found, anyway. Ramsbottom said there wasn't a trace of Jodie's DNA on it. Just a hammer in a sink—clean as a whistle."

Did that rule Stuart out? It ruled out his hammer, at least.

"What about the other stuff? The note? The guitar string?"

"I don't know *everything*, dear."

"Can I have that in writing?" Claire joked.

Janet pouted. "That's unfair. I've mellowed."

"Only because I'm not single anymore," Claire said as she wrestled the broken gate open, "and I've given you two ready-made step-grandchildren."

Janet smiled warmly. "And it was rather nice to skip the toddler phase. Oh, you were so *fussy*!" She fished the keys from her coat pocket and held them out. "Go on, you open it."

"I'll pass on that honour."

Janet tutted but unlocked the door herself. It swung open, revealing the dim, hollow interior. The chill in the air, the fresh plaster—it was all the same. But something heavier hung in the atmosphere now. Amelia had been right. A ghost seemed to linger.

"Now then." Janet clapped her hands, standing squarely in the kitchen, right where Jodie's body had been found. "Ramsbottom said they sped up the process to get this back to you. Crime scene cleaners have been through, but clearly, they didn't do much." She glanced around. "Where exactly was the body?"

"It doesn't matter," Claire murmured, her gaze fixed on the floorboards. The bloodstain had been scrubbed away, but she could still *feel* it.

"Well, can we at least get some heat going?" Janet spun out the long cord from Henry. "If we're scrubbing this place top to bottom, I don't want to shiver. Where's the thermostat?"

"Under the stairs," Claire said, her eyes drifting upstairs.

She hesitated, suddenly unsure if they were alone. When the steps creaked faintly under her weight, she froze. Then Janet's sharp gasp cut through the silence.

"*Claire?*" Janet called from the corridor. "You wouldn't happen to be keeping a bloody candlestick wrapped in a rag under the stairs for any reason, would you?"

Claire rushed over. Sure enough, there was an ornate brass candlestick, its base marked with a sticker from Lilac Gifts, a shop in the square.

"Funnily enough, no," Claire said, her throat dry. Her gaze lingered on the candlestick. "I think we've found the murder weapon. It still smells fresh."

Janet exhaled through flared nostrils. "How Ramsbottom still has his job, I'll never understand. Under the stairs is the *first* place I'd check." She reached for the candlestick but hesitated, her better judgment prevailing. With a sharp sigh, she straightened. "Well, it looks like we're not cleaning tonight. Which of us is calling Ramsbottom?"

Claire stared up the staircase as another creak echoed from above. Was it the house settling? Or someone moving?

"You do it," Claire said, her voice tight. "I'll be right back."

While Janet berated Ramsbottom over the phone, Claire crept upstairs. The landing was still, the faint scent of cleaning products lingering from the crime scene team's work. Four bedrooms and a bathroom, all freshly plastered, waiting to be decorated. Three doors stood open, but one was shut.

She clenched the handle, braced herself, and pushed it open.

Inside, Lucy was curled up on the brand-new carpet—a gift from Janet, who 'couldn't bear the thought' of Claire and Ryan walking on anything cheap first thing in the morning. Lucy's eyes snapped open, and she startled, scrambling back until her shoulders hit the wall. Her fingers fumbled for the window latch, her wide eyes never leaving Claire.

"You don't want to take your chances jumping," Claire said as calmly as she could muster. "Even if you hit the grass, it'll be frozen solid."

"I'm sorry," Lucy whispered, her voice breaking. "I was tired, and I didn't know where else to go."

"It's alright." Claire hesitated, then stepped into the room, keeping her tone gentle. "Would you like a cup of tea?"

Lucy shook her head, suspicion flaring in her eyes. After a long pause, she said quietly, "I prefer coffee."

Claire's lips curved into a small smile. "Yeah? Me too."

CHAPTER SEVEN

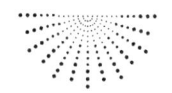

Claire ushered Lucy into her parents' house. The place was spotless—almost too perfect. Every surface gleamed under the glare of the lamps, every decoration precisely in its place.

Lucy's wide-eyed gaze flitted over the Christmas wonderland sitting room. Claire shifted uncomfortably, aware of how extravagant it must have seemed through Lucy's eyes. The house felt like a museum, an exhibition of her mother's obsessive order and her father's earnings as a career detective. A standard Claire had neither tried nor wanted to meet.

"Sorry," Claire said, her cheeks warming. "It's a bit much, I know."

"It's nice. Reminds me of my grandad's house. He was house proud."

Claire offered a faint smile and led her through to the kitchen. Laughter greeted her, warm and unexpected.

At the table, Granny Greta sat with Claire's father, a bottle of whisky and two crystal tumblers between them. The Scrabble board lay abandoned, its tiles scattered, as their conversation took precedence over the game.

Greta's face lit up as Claire walked in. Short and round, like all the Harris women, she radiated an effortless warmth that made her one of Claire's favourite people—not just in the family, but in the world. Of course, that was when Greta wasn't off gallivanting on one of her many cruises.

"Tell Claire what you just told me, Mum," Alan said.

Greta stood, greeting Claire with a kiss on the cheek.

"Good to see you, love," she said warmly. "And who's your friend?"

"This is Lucy."

She hesitated to add more, unsure how much Lucy wanted to share. Greta studied Lucy with her usual keen gaze before settling back into her chair.

"I was just telling your father about my new lodger," Greta said, topping up her whisky with a splash. "Took him in this afternoon. Met him at the chippy, of all places. He said he had nowhere to go, and you know how I like to rent out the spare bedroom when I can. Pays for my cruises."

Claire's stomach flipped. "Who is he?"

"Some young chap called Richard."

"*Ricky?*" Lucy's voice jumped, her eyes widening.

Claire's mind flashed back to Maria's words in the café, the pointed comment about Ricky and Lucy's feelings—past tense, Lucy had insisted. But now, the spark in her eyes told a different story.

"That's him," Greta said, her expression curious. "Friend of yours?"

Lucy hesitated, then gave a slight nod.

"Well, now I'm not so sure about letting him stay," Greta said, her lips puckering. "Not if he's mixed up in this murder business, according to Alan."

"*No*," Lucy said quickly. "He isn't. Ricky wouldn't. He wasn't even there. He ran off the night before Jodie died and didn't come back. I haven't seen him since."

"I saw him," Claire said, her tone measured. "He was across the cul-de-sac, watching while the police were investigating the scene."

Greta leaned forward, intrigued. "And who is he? He seems nice enough."

"He *is*," Lucy insisted, then hesitated. "But he's troubled."

"Troubled how?" Alan asked, his voice calm but probing.

Lucy shrugged, as though it were obvious. "He's insecure. But he's a natural leader, he just needs to step up. He used to be in a band—lead guitarist. They kicked him out because he wanted to write deeper songs, ones about the world and real things. He didn't want to waste his talent on meaningless stuff. You should hear him play guitar." A faint smile brightened her face, but she shook it away. "It was *his* idea that we all stick together."

"We all?" Claire asked.

"The squatters," Lucy clarified. "It's our band."

"You play music?" Greta asked, suddenly animated. "Know any Elvis?"

"No."

"You don't know *Elvis*?" Greta exclaimed. "What are they teaching the kids these days?"

"I do, but we don't play music." Lucy's tone flattened. "It's just a band of people. Friends. I met Maria first at the job centre, then Ricky in the pub, then Stuart in the park. We were all down on our luck and didn't know how to get out of it. Ricky thought we'd do better together. So, we always move as a group. Survival. The four of us."

"There's five," Claire pointed out. "*Was* five. Who was the latest addition?"

Lucy stiffened, her eyes darting between Alan and Greta. She retreated into herself.

Greta, ever intuitive, leaned back and drummed the table. "Alan," she said, "why don't you show me that new chair you've got in your potting shed? The one you were telling me about?"

Alan blinked, puzzled for a moment, then caught on. "Ah, yes. The chair. It's a real beauty."

Claire stifled a smile. She knew full well that the 'new chair' was the same creaky office chair Alan had pulled from a skip when she was ten. She gave Greta a grateful nod as the pair left the room, their voices trailing off down the garden path.

"Make yourself comfy," Claire said, pulling out a chair at the table. "I'll make the coffee, but help yourself to the whisky."

"Coffee is fine," Lucy replied with a polite smile.

Claire spooned instant coffee into two mugs, poured in boiling water, and returned to the table. She slid one mug to Lucy, who wrapped her hands around it, letting the warmth seep into her fingers. She took a small sip, savouring it like it was nectar.

"It was Jodie, wasn't it?" Claire asked, blowing gently on her coffee. "The newest arrival to your band?"

Lucy froze. Her fingers tightened around the mug, her gaze locked on the dark liquid. After a long pause, she nodded.

"She was your sister."

Another pause. Another nod.

"We found a candlestick under the stairs," Claire said, tilting her head. "Do you know anything about that?"

Lucy's eyes darted up, a flicker of something crossing her face—recognition? She seemed to visualise it, piecing something together. Then she shook her head and took another sip.

"You lost your job at the gallery," Claire pressed. "For forgery?"

Lucy nodded slowly. "Jodie got me that job. She wrote me a fake CV. The money was good, though. That's all we needed. That's all Jodie ever wanted—for us to have enough."

Claire noticed the paint splattered across Lucy's clothes, fresh streaks mingling with older stains. She thought of the smudges of paint Ramsbottom had found on Jodie's jacket.

"Do you paint?" Claire asked.

Lucy nodded, but didn't elaborate.

"Jodie took Stuart's money," Claire pivoted, sipping her hot coffee. "Five hundred pounds, wasn't it? She promised to double it."

Lucy's lips twitched. "She wasn't going to double it. Not unless her lucky horse came in at the races."

"Ah."

"She did try…" Lucy trailed off, her tone sceptical. "But she struggled. Always did. Our dad raised us, and he wasn't like your dad. Your dad's got his little shed at the bottom of the garden. Ours had stolen cars waiting to be broken down. Jodie learned from him." Her gaze misted over as she travelled further back. "I had this little paint set. Stole it from the corner shop. Just chalky watercolours and I only had old envelopes to paint on, but that's all I'd do. All day. I'd flip through magazines people threw away and paint what I saw. Nobody ever bothered me when I was painting. I covered the walls with them. Dad called me a parrot for copying, but Jodie said that's how all the best artists start."

Glad that Lucy was opening up, Claire was scared to push too far. Still, she had questions, and Lucy had slipped through her fingers several times.

"What about the forgeries at the gallery?" Claire asked. "The ones you were fired for?"

"I don't want to talk about it."

"That's fine," Claire said gently, though it wasn't. Every question felt like another door slamming in her face. She tried again. "The police think Jodie died around six in the morning. Where were you?"

"Asleep," Lucy said. "Jodie always said I could sleep through the end of the world."

Claire narrowed her eyes. "Who else was with you?"

"Maria," Lucy replied. "Jodie always liked her own room if she could get it. The men slept separately. Jodie used to say I shouldn't give people the wrong impression."

"The wrong impression?" Claire echoed.

Lucy didn't respond, staring into her coffee.

"What was the group like before Jodie?" Claire pressed.

"We had this flat," she said, frowning as though the memory of it hurt to think about. "Maria got it through the council. It was only supposed to be for one, but we all chipped in what we could. Then Jodie's girlfriend left her, and she had to start over with nothing. She took our savings pot. A little sugar pot we kept it in. When we couldn't pay the rent and ignored the letters, we got a visit. They kicked us out. We've been hopping around ever since, finding houses that look abandoned. If we'd known you were about to move in—"

Claire raised a hand. "Fair point," she said. "The state it's in, it does look abandoned. Might as well be. I had a neighbour who lived there once—Mrs Beaton. Mad as a box of frogs. She had all these cats she couldn't look after—"

A furious banging at the front door cut her off, followed by the sound of someone letting themselves in. Claire startled, springing to her feet. Lucy froze, her mug hovering mid-air.

Claire rushed into the hallway to see Maria, her face flushed and furious, poking her head into the sitting room before marching straight through to the kitchen. She stopped short at the sight of Lucy and jabbed an accusatory finger at her.

"Let's go," Maria demanded. "You don't have to say anything to these people."

"We were just talking," Claire said. "Sit down, and I'll make you—"

"*Exploiting* her, more like," Maria snapped, flapping her hand impatiently for Lucy to move. "Extracting information. Trying to get her to confess to something she didn't do."

"That's not it at all," Claire protested, turning to Lucy for support. But Lucy drained the last of her coffee and slipped around Maria, her head down. "Maria, I can tell you're protective of her."

"*Protective?*" Maria let out a humourless laugh. "You've *no* idea what we've been through."

She grabbed Lucy's arm and guided her down the hallway. Claire followed them to the doorstep, her stomach churning.

"What did you mean when you said Jodie had dirt on everyone and wasn't afraid to use it?" Claire called, her voice trembling. "That sounds like blackmail to me."

Maria froze, turning slowly. "You *were* listening in the café," she said, her eyes narrowing. "Why do you care so much?"

"A woman was murdered where my new kitchen is supposed to go."

"Yeah?" Maria whispered, glancing back at 1 Birch Close. She leaned in closer, her voice low enough that Lucy wouldn't hear. "Good riddance." Straightening, her tone turned brisk. "C'mon, Lucy. I explained our situation to the nice man at the B&B. He's given us a room for the night. Hot showers included."

"I just want to know what happened," Claire called after them. "I won't give up until I know. Whether the police find out or I do it myself."

"Then it's Stuart you should be talking to," Maria replied. "He didn't think I could hear him last night, but before Jodie and Ricky came to blows and Ricky legged it, Stuart told Jodie that if she didn't pay back the money by sunrise, she'd be a dead woman."

Without waiting for Claire's reaction, Maria tugged Lucy across the cul-de-sac. Claire stood on the doorstep, her thoughts racing. Stuart had threatened to kill Jodie before sunrise—and that was exactly what had happened.

Back inside, Claire hurried through the quiet kitchen, out the back door, and down the garden path to the shed. Greta and Alan's chuckles filled the space, his secret whisky stash pulled out of the bottom drawer in the potting desk. He'd brought out biscuits too.

Greta was mid-story, chuckling as she said, "I was just reminding your father of when he got his first gardening shears. He cut the heads off all the flowers in the garden to 'test' them."

"I was seven," Alan protested with a grin.

Claire managed a laugh, but it felt hollow. She helped herself to an almost frozen chocolate digestive, but it was like chewing on dust. Her unsettled expression must have caught her father's attention because his smile faded.

"What did you find out, little one?"

Claire sat on her plant pot, weighing everything she'd just heard—Lucy's evasive explanations, Maria's abrupt arrival and deflection, her pointed accusation of Stuart. The puzzle pieces didn't fit. Every answer seemed to sprout two new questions.

"I found out," she said finally, "that I don't trust Lucy or Maria. And the one person who seems to know what's going on more than anyone—Maria—seems to be the last person who'll want to talk to me."

"Well, that's not the best situation," Greta said, finishing her whisky in one smooth motion. She set the glass down with a clink, her expression turning thoughtful. "But my new lodger should be out of the bath if you want to talk to him?"

As they crossed the cul-de-sac, a sudden clatter made them both turn. Carol was by her wheelie bin, tossing something inside. Claire recognised the pine wreath, the same one that had fallen off when Carol slammed the door after berating Claire for 'letting' the squatters in.

Carol spotted them, her face hardening before she went back inside, slamming the door with unnecessary force once again. This time, there was no wreath to fall off, but the echo of the slam was impactful enough.

The message was clear: Carol blamed Claire for everything happening next door.

At 1 Birch Close, Ramsbottom and his officers were back, with Janet keeping a sharp watch over them as they assessed under the stairs.

"What's Carol's problem?" Greta tutted. "Miserable goat."

"I don't know," Claire said, watching the house, "but I'd like to find out."

"Well, she reminds me of your mother."

"My mother has mellowed."

Greta snorted. "According to whom?"

"My mother."

"Ha! Sounds about right." Greta chuckled, looping her arm through Claire's as they strolled down the lane. "So, this Ricky character—should I be worried about inviting a potential murderer into my home?"

Claire squinted towards the distant lights of the village, hoping the lodger hadn't scarpered already.

"That," she said, "is another thing I'd like to find out."

CHAPTER EIGHT

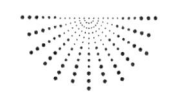

Greta's kitchen, tucked at the back of her small terraced cottage, was a swirling mix of steamy air and the smell of frying sausages. Ricky stood at the oven, a towel precariously wrapped around his narrow waist, water dripping from his lanky frame. Scars crisscrossed his chest and arms, faint but unmistakable, like fragments of a story he wasn't ready to tell—and Claire wasn't sure she wanted to ask about.

"Claire, right?" he said, his voice neutral but strained. "Your gran's been really nice. Don't know what I'd do without her."

"She's a saint," Claire replied, leaning against the doorframe. "But I'm not here for small talk."

Greta appeared behind her, Spud yapping furiously at

Ricky. The little Yorkshire Terrier lunged like he was ready to take a bite out of him.

"Spud!" Greta snapped. "It's the sausages, isn't it? He's got a nose for them." She grabbed the lead from the back of the door. "Come on, Spud. Time for a lap around Starfall Park so we can all have some peace." She glanced meaningfully at Claire as she left. "I'll give you two a moment."

Ricky sighed, muttering under his breath as he poked at the sausages with a fork. The polite smile dropped the second Greta was out of earshot.

"So," Claire said, stepping further into the kitchen. "About the guitar string they found at the scene—"

"Right," Ricky interrupted, his tone sharp. "Let me guess. You're here to blame me? Frame me? Think I'm just another squatter who deserves what's coming?"

"That's not what I'm doing. But I know you and Jodie argued."

"And you saw me leave, didn't you?"

"I saw you come back," Claire corrected, her tone firm. "Through the fog. After she'd been murdered."

"*After*," he repeated, shaking the frying pan. The oil hissed and spat, flecking his skin, though he didn't seem to notice. "And so what? I wanted to check on Lucy, saw the police, and ran. I thought someone had grassed. Squatting's not exactly easy, especially with Jodie screwing everything up. Control freak."

"Controlling who?" Claire asked, stepping closer. "The group? Or just Lucy?"

Ricky didn't answer. He jabbed at the sausages, his silence enough for Claire to suspect it was both.

"Lucy said you were a good guitar player," Claire pressed. "Where is it?"

"How would I know? I went back for it, but I didn't want to be lugging it around. Jodie threw me out again."

"You didn't get on with her?"

"None of us did," Ricky snapped. "Jodie…"

"Had dirt on everyone?" Claire finished for him.

He hesitated, the fork in his hand hovering mid-air. "As it happens, yeah."

"So, what did she have on you?"

Ricky turned off the hob, grabbing a sausage straight from the pan. He bit into it, chewing through the heat, taking his time.

"Jodie hated me because I loved Lucy," he said, surprising her with the admission. "Lucy wasn't allowed to love me."

Claire frowned. "She wasn't *allowed*?"

"Because Jodie only saw one thing when she looked at her," he spat. "A cash cow. A meal ticket. You know she's a genius, right?"

"Lucy?"

"Give her a paintbrush and watch what she can do," he said. "Jodie used that talent any way she could."

"The forgeries?"

"I don't know about that," Ricky said quickly, but there was something in his eyes—protection or self-preservation. Maybe both. "I know she loved that gallery job. That was Lucy's ticket out. Jodie saw it as hers. And when she didn't want to share, she took it from her."

"Jodie got her fired?" Claire asked.

Ricky nodded, stabbing another sausage. "The forgeries were identical. Nobody knew they weren't originals until someone grassed to the gallery."

"Original what?" Claire prompted.

"Paintings," Ricky said like it was obvious. "She could mimic anything. She just *saw*."

"Saw?" Claire repeated.

"That's what I said, isn't it?" he mumbled, taking another bite. He glanced up, his eyes narrowing. "But Jodie was the leader, so her word was law."

"That's not what Lucy says."

Ricky frowned, his hand pausing mid-reach for another sausage. "What are you talking about?"

"She said you were their leader before Jodie came along. That you looked after them," Claire said, tilting her head. "But from what I've seen, Jodie was in charge."

"Because she forced her way in," Ricky snapped. He jabbed the fork at the plate, the fork shrieking against the porcelain. "We were doing fine before she turned up. We were almost happy, making our way. She ruined it all."

Claire hesitated, watching as his tense expression softened into something more vulnerable.

"Do you know why I fell in love with Lucy?" he asked quietly, his voice barely above a whisper.

Claire shook her head.

"Because she was *always* smiling," Ricky said, no trace of a smile on his face. "No matter how hard things got, she'd find something to laugh about. She kept us going."

Claire's chest tightened. Given how dour and withdrawn Lucy had been lately, hearing that broke her heart a little.

"Look, I've kept my cool because your gran's been nice," he said, his tone hardening. "But I don't like all these questions. So, if you don't mind." He gestured at his plate with the fork. "Clear off, and let me eat in peace. This is the first hot meal I've had in days."

Claire opened the fridge, pulled out a ketchup bottle, and handed it to him. He snatched it without thanks, squeezing a generous dollop onto the plate in thick lines.

"I heard that Stuart said he was going to kill Jodie by sunrise," Claire said from the doorway. "Did you hear that?"

"Nope."

"Anything else to add?"

"Nope."

Claire sighed. "Thanks for your time."

Maria had claimed that Stuart and Jodie's

confrontation happened before Ricky left. That meant either Ricky wasn't in the room at the time, or someone was lying. Either way, Stuart was the missing link—and unlike the others, he hadn't been around.

She paused at the door. "Any idea where I'd find Stuart?"

"Nope," Ricky said again, finishing the last sausage. "He goes where the work is."

Claire stepped outside as Greta returned from her walk around the park with Spud. Behind her, the gallery next to the second-hand clothes shop had shut for the day, spotlights lighting up the paintings in the darkened room. She needed to visit to ask about Lucy and her forged paintings.

"Well?" Greta asked. "Should I sleep with one eye open?"

Claire bent down to scratch Spud's ears, not wanting to alarm her gran but also not wanting to lie to her.

"Try both," she said.

"*That* bad?"

"I don't know," Claire admitted. "Not yet. Just watch out."

"Likewise," Greta replied, squeezing her arm gently. "*Likewise*."

The cheer of a Christmas party flowed from The Hesketh Arms as Claire walked across the square with brisk steps. She glanced at the gym housed in the old library building, but Ryan wouldn't be finished for another hour. Until then, she couldn't afford to wait around.

She passed the row of shops adjacent to hers, their Christmas decorations so dazzlingly bright they could probably be seen from space. She paused outside *Lilac Gifts*, cupping her hands around her face to block out the reflections on the glass. Among the glittering displays of ornaments and candles, something caught her eye.

The candlestick from under the stairs.

It was unmistakable.

Straightening, her breath fogging the glass, Claire made a mental note to ask Gwyneth, the shop's owner, about it tomorrow. If anyone could remember who bought the candlestick, it'd be her.

"Claire?" The voice startled her, and she turned to see Sally perched on the doorstep of the candle shop. "Your shop's over here. Lost?"

"Window shopping," Claire replied, hopping off the path and onto the road. "What are you doing?"

Sally held up a bottle of red wine. "Waiting. Hoping. Did you talk to him?"

"Him?"

"Damon," Sally said, exasperated. "I mean, not that I'm *obsessed* or anything, but you didn't, did you?"

"No," Claire admitted. "He ran off after work. Told me he was busy."

"Me too, but he's not in his flat, and he always tells me what he's doing. I don't care half the time, but he *always* tells me. And now I feel like some crazy stalker."

"Let's take this upstairs," Claire said, unlocking the shop. "I think I know which boxes the glasses are in."

They passed through the dark shop to the small flat above. It had been home to Claire for the past few years, and had somehow turned into an unofficial storage room that she, Ryan, and the kids had been navigating their lives around for weeks. Boxes filled every available space—moving boxes, stock boxes, boxes filled with boxes. It had been out of control for a while.

"Oh dear," Sally said, glancing around. Sally's house in 'Upper Northash' on the other side of the park could have fronted an interior design magazine. "I'm guessing your mum hasn't seen this?"

"And she won't." Claire laughed. "You can see why I've been so eager to get out of here."

They shifted a few boxes and cleared a spot on the sofa before flopping down, staring at the space where the TV had been.

"Remember when you first viewed this place?" Sally said, rolling her head along the back of the sofa to face

Claire. "Back when you couldn't afford it—when this flat and the shop were everything you ever wanted?"

"And then so much more happened."

"I still can't believe you and Ryan are a thing. You and Ryan from *school*. You've loved him since we were kids, not that he noticed." At that, Sally burst into tears, burying her face in her hands. "I think I'm losing Damon, Claire. I can *feel* it. He's pulling away, sneaking around. I can't go through *this* again."

Claire reached behind the sofa, dug through a box, and pulled out two wine glasses, unwrapping them with care. She poured the wine, handing one to Sally.

"Damon isn't the type of man to stray," Claire assured her, "if that's what you're thinking."

"All men *can* and *will*," Sally muttered after a slurp. "Except Ryan, of course. And your dad."

"*And* Damon," Claire added firmly. "For one, he knows I'd kill him if I found out."

"Oh, mate." Sally blinked at her, a hint of a smile breaking through. "You would?"

"Without a second thought," Claire said with conviction. "But I can say that confidently because I *know* he wouldn't."

Claire hated seeing her friend like this.

"Knowing Damon," Claire said in her most reassuring voice, "he's off doing something tragically geeky and he's too embarrassed to talk about."

Sally sniffed, her tears calming. "You think so?"

"I do."

"Look at me." She scrubbed at her tears with the back of her hand. "My mum's got the kids, a man is ignoring my texts, and here we are, drinking wine. We've been here before."

They both laughed, the sound cutting through the worry. It had once been a common occurrence—sometimes weekly—but there'd been fewer tears since Sally's divorce.

"Some things never change," Sally said.

"But plenty does," Claire reminded her.

"Like your house."

"My house," Claire echoed. "Doesn't feel like it yet."

"It will. It's just a building. You make a house a home. The people… the feeling… the love…" Her voice cracked, and she started crying again. "No. I'm a big girl. How are we almost *forty*, Claire? How'd that sneak up on us?"

"I don't know, but I'd like it to slow down."

"I'm sorry," Sally said, dabbing at her eyes. "You're the one going through it right now, aren't you? I'm so selfish, as usual."

"Sally, it's fine," Claire said, setting her glass down. "That's why I'm here. Vent, cry, turn up on my doorstep with wine—just make sure it's the *right* doorstep next time. I haven't lived here for at least a whole day."

They laughed again, and for a moment, it really was like old times—not just the flat-above-the-shop times, but teenage times. It was always like that with Sally. No matter how much they changed or how far they drifted, they always ended up leaning on each other when it mattered.

Sally looked at her wine glass, then at the bottle, and sighed. "You know what? I'm not in the mood to drown my sorrows anymore. Tomorrow's headache is putting me off."

"And *that's* how we know we're almost forty," Claire said, pouring the rest of her glass into a plant that had already given up on life.

Sally took one last sip, and followed suit.

Claire leaned back against the sofa, her finger tracing the rim of her empty glass. Sally tucked her legs underneath herself, her eyes red raw from crying but now sharper, more focused.

"Alright," Sally said, sitting up straighter, determination cutting through the haze. "No more wallowing. What's going on with you? What do you know?"

Claire exhaled, rubbing the bridge of her nose underneath her glasses. What did she know? Too much, and nothing at all.

"It's not about what I know," she said carefully, "it's about what I think. And I'm not even sure that's right."

"Spill it anyway," Sally pressed. "Sometimes saying it out loud helps."

Claire reached for a sheet of paper from a stack on the coffee table—last term's timetable for Northash Primary School. She flipped it over and dug a pen out of the fruit bowl, which had never actually held fruit.

"Alright, let's start with Lucy," Claire said, pen poised over the paper. "I found her upstairs in the house earlier, right above where her sister was murdered. I was so surprised to see her that I didn't notice how strange that was until I just said it now."

"See!" Sally said, tapping the paper for emphasis. "You've got to hear yourself. That *is* strange."

"There's something about her that doesn't sit right," Claire continued. "She's so detached most of the time, but then she has these moments where you can tell she's holding back. I found paint on her clothes earlier, and Jodie had fresh paint on her."

"She's a painter?"

"A mimic and a genius, according to Ricky," Claire said, scribbling the details down. "And she lost her job at the gallery because of forgeries. Though I don't know what she was forging, and the gallery owner wouldn't tell Ryan."

Sally let out a low whistle. "You think this girl could kill?"

"I don't know," Claire admitted. "She doesn't *seem* like

the type to kill someone, but maybe it was self-defence? I overheard her saying she hated 'her', and I'm sure it was about her sister. I just don't trust her."

"Okay," Sally said, nodding. "Who's next?"

"Maria," Claire said, writing down the name. "She's a piece of work and protective of Lucy to the point I can barely get close enough to talk to her. And even when Maria isn't there, it's like Lucy can feel her watching. Earlier, Maria let herself into my parents' house to accuse me of trying to manipulate Lucy into a confession."

"Defensive much?"

"Exactly," Claire agreed. "And she said, 'good riddance' about Jodie. Who says that about someone who's just died? She didn't hide that she disliked Jodie, but the way she reacted when she saw her dead, it was like she'd lost a friend."

"You think she faked her reaction?"

"Possibly?" Claire said, though she wasn't sure. "She admitted that Jodie had dirt on everyone."

"Motive?"

"Maybe to protect Lucy? Or to stop Jodie from exposing her secrets. Either way, I'm in her bad books."

"She sounds like a nightmare," Sally said, tapping the paper. "Who's next?"

"Stuart's the most obvious suspect," Claire admitted. "He openly threatened Jodie—Maria said she heard him tell Jodie she'd be a dead man if she didn't pay him back by sunrise. And his hammer was found at the scene."

"Sounds like a slam dunk."

"Except the hammer didn't kill Jodie," Claire said, frustration creeping into her voice. "We found a bloody candlestick under the stairs, so that's the likely murder weapon. But Stuart's disappeared. He hasn't been around like the others."

"Sketchy," Sally agreed. "Who's next?"

"Ricky," Claire said, frowning. "He's complicated. He admitted he argued with Jodie and said Jodie hated him because he was in love with Lucy. Jodie didn't want anyone else having control over her."

Sally's eyebrows shot up. "Control? What kind of control?"

"Ricky thinks Jodie saw her as a cash cow."

"That's disgusting, but if Ricky cared about her, wouldn't he want to get rid of Jodie?"

"Maybe," Claire agreed with a nod. "But he's cagey. I can't tell if he's hiding something about himself or protecting Lucy."

"Is that all of them?"

"The squatters, yes," Claire said, tapping her pen against the paper. "But there's also Carol, my neighbour. She's a wildcard—claimed she was in bed with Kris the morning of the murder, but my mum saw her outside talking to someone long before sunrise. She hated the squatters and didn't bother hiding it."

"Carol Hodgkinson?" Sally whispered, wide-eyed. "She's a nightmare. I sold a house to her daughter a few years ago, and Carol interfered the whole time. Talked down to her husband too."

"I've heard them arguing multiple times," Claire said, jotting down notes until the page ran out of space. "He said something that made me think Carol made up her alibi. She's been acting off all day. Mind you, she's never been friendly to me, but now she's glaring, slamming doors. I can't figure out why she'd want to kill Jodie other than disliking her for squatting next door."

"Could that be motive enough?" Sally asked.

Claire sighed, setting the sheet on the coffee table. "Maybe. But they *all* had reasons to hate Jodie. *I* didn't like her. But so far, only one person was overheard threatening to kill her. I don't suppose you know a man called Stuart? He's a builder—tall, in his fifties?"

Sally shook her head. "Sorry, mate."

"Then that's what I need to focus on tomorrow. If he's still in Northash, I'll find him." Looking towards the window, she added, "Someone somewhere will know where he's gone."

"You'll figure it out, mate." Sally reached over and squeezed her arm. "You always do."

"And so will you," Claire said, sliding off the sofa. At the window, she noticed Ryan turning off the lights at the gym. "I'll talk to Damon tomorrow. Find out what's going on."

"Don't tell him I sent you."

"I'll be subtle," Claire assured her. "I want to know what's going on with him too. I think he tried to tell me the other day, but I was too busy." She sighed, remembering how she'd dismissed him. At the time, Damon hadn't seemed too bothered, but now she wondered if things with Sally might have gone differently if she'd been able to confirm—or deny—Sally's theory. "For now, you're welcome to stay here tonight."

Sally dragged herself off the sofa. "I'll head home. Early viewings tomorrow. What about you?"

"I'm going home too," Claire said, holding up a hand when Ryan spotted her from across the square.

"Well, good luck tomorrow." Sally grabbed her bag and slung it over her shoulder. "And Claire?"

"Yeah?" Claire said, still watching Ryan through the window as he locked up the gym.

"Thanks for tonight. I know I'm a bit of a mess sometimes, but you've always got my back, and I'm grateful."

Claire pulled her into a hug. "Always. Now go home and get some rest. Damon's probably planning a surprise *Dungeons & Dragons* campaign."

"If he is, I'm making you roll the dice for me because I *still* don't understand how to play."

"And you think I do?"

The friends parted with laughter, and Claire grabbed her coat, switching off the lights before stepping outside into the cold night air. She crossed the square and headed to Ryan by the gym doors.

"You're early," she said, tucking her hands into her pockets.

"Thought I'd lock up before anyone else wandered in looking for a Christmas miracle set of abs," Ryan said, wrapping his arm around her. "You okay?"

"Is that your way of saying I look knackered?" Claire replied, leaning into his warm side. "Because yes, I am."

They set off to the cul-de-sac as Claire's mind whirred through what she'd discussed with Sally: Lucy's paint-streaked clothes, Maria's accusations, Stuart's threats, Ricky's defensiveness, Carol's questionable alibi. The pieces pointed somewhere, but the destination was maddeningly unclear.

Claire paused at her parents' gate, turning to look at their empty house. Somewhere in the distance, a church bell chimed the hour.

Ryan followed her gaze. "What's on your mind?"

"I was going to ask you the same thing. You're quiet."

Ryan shrugged, stuffing his hands into his jacket pockets. "Just tired."

"Don't give me that," she said. "This is me, Ryan. What's going on?"

He looked at her, his mouth twitching in a half-smile. "You don't let anything slide, do you?"

"Not when it's you. Come on, spill. Is it about the gallery job?"

"Yeah. It's just a lot."

Claire nodded, giving him space to continue.

"I've spent so long in the gym, you know?" Ryan began, his words slow, deliberate. "It's what I do. It's what people expect. But it's not really me. Not completely, anyway."

Claire leaned beside him, tilting her head. "You mean the art."

"Yeah," he said, his voice barely above a whisper. "The art. It's always been *my* thing. But the idea of doing it—*really* doing it—it scares the hell out of me."

"Why?" she asked gently.

"Because it matters," Ryan said, meeting her eyes. "The gym's rewarding, but it's just work. Lifting weights and counting reps doesn't ask much of me. Art is different. It's *personal*. It's what my mum taught me. If I fail at that, it's like failing at who I am."

"You won't fail," Claire said, her voice steady. "You've already sold pieces. People love your work, Ryan. I love your work."

He smiled at that, but it didn't quite reach his eyes. "You're biased."

"I'm *honest*," she countered. "You've got something special. And this gallery job is time around art, time to make art, talk about it, live it. Isn't that what you've always wanted?"

Ryan looked down, scuffing his shoe against the frost-bitten pavement. "Maybe. But what if it's not? What if it's just some romanticised idea I've clung to since I was a chubby teenager sketching in the back of Spanish cafés?"

"It's not," Claire said firmly. "I knew you before then, remember? Art wasn't just a hobby for you. It was everything. The gym, the reinventing yourself—that's great, but it's not the whole picture. You know that."

Ryan sighed, leaning his head back to look at the sky. "I don't want to decide yet. It feels too *big*."

They stood in silence for a moment, the air between them still and steady. Finally, Claire straightened and turned towards the house.

"You don't have to decide now," she said, opening the front door. "Why don't we get an early night? I have a feeling tomorrow is going to be a big day."

CHAPTER NINE

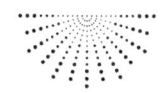

The bell above the door tinkled as Claire stepped into Lilac Gifts. The shop was a dazzling wonderland of Christmas cheer, every surface overflowing with greeting cards and festive trinkets.

Behind the counter stood Gwyneth, once affectionately known in the village as the local 'Marilyn Monroe.' Her platinum blonde hair was styled to perfection, her beauty mark firmly in place. Clad in a festive red cardigan and pearl earrings, she exuded an effortless, timeless glamour.

"Claire! Darling," Gwyneth greeted, her smile as dazzling as the ornaments on display. "What brings you here on a Sunday? Shouldn't you be in your shop?"

"It's Damon's turn this week," Claire said, unzipping

her thick coat. "Our first Christmas opening the extra day, but it's still quiet."

"Hmm, yes, it can be. But just you wait until later," Gwyneth said with a knowing tap of her nose. "So, what can I do for you? Christmas decorations? Cards? Reed diffuser?"

"Actually, I needed to ask you something." She plucked the brass candlestick from the display she'd noticed through the window last night. "Do you know if you've sold one of these recently?"

"Hmm." Gwyneth drummed her red nails on the counter. "Off the top of my head, I can't say I have. I've had that design in stock for years. Let me check the receipts."

She disappeared into the back, leaving Claire to wander along the aisles. Her fingers brushed the soft velvet of a ribboned gift box as she waited. She still didn't know what to get Ryan for Christmas. He wasn't a trinkets kind of person. Neither was she, aside from her candles.

When Gwyneth returned, she held a small receipt in hand.

"Looks like we sold one two days ago on Friday morning," she said, peering through her reading glasses without putting them on. "The customer paid for gift wrapping. That's unusual for a candlestick, but perhaps it was a Christmas present."

"Do you know who bought it?" Claire asked.

"I wasn't working that day, and this doesn't tell me much since they paid in cash." She considered, drumming her nails again. "Becky was on shift. I can ask her if she remembers, but I can't promise anything."

"That would be great, thank you," Claire said, her mind racing. Had the murderer bought a candlestick from a local shop, had it gift-wrapped, and then unwrapped it just to clobber someone over the head? The one they'd found under the stairs did have the Lilac Gifts sticker on the bottom.

"Is everything alright, Claire?" Gwyneth gave her a curious look. "You seem stressed?"

Claire forced a smile. "Christmas," she lied, unwilling to admit Gwyneth's shop might have sold a murder weapon without more facts. "You know how it is."

"Don't I ever," Gwyneth said with a laugh. "Well, if Becky remembers anything, I'll pop by to let you know."

Claire thanked her and stepped back out into the cold.

A brass candlestick.

Sold on Friday.

Gift-wrapped.

There was every chance the wrapped candlestick was waiting patiently under someone's tree, while the one that killed Jodie had been bought weeks, months, or even years ago.

But the fact one was sold the morning before the murder?

It had to mean something.

Back in the candle shop, Damon would be twiddling his thumbs—or reading a graphic novel, as was often the case—now the lunchtime rush had passed. Claire wanted to catch him before he had too much time to stew, but she spotted DI Ramsbottom standing near the burger van in the Christmas market. The scent of sizzling meat and onions curled through the air, rumbling her stomach. Ramsbottom, however, looked preoccupied, clutching a folder in one hand while he waited for his food.

"Miss Harris!" he called, catching sight of her. He waved her over with the folder. "You've got a knack for these things. Spare a moment?"

"What is it?"

"I want your thoughts on something." He opened the folder and pulled out a photocopy of the charred note they'd found at the scene. "What do you make of this?"

Claire leaned closer, scanning the faint scrawl. Somewhere nearby, someone was hammering. Shutting out the din, she focused on the initials, recognising them as the ones Ramsbottom had read aloud at the crime scene. It wasn't much, but it was something:

- C.H. £2000
- L.R. £200 (settled)

- R.G. £10,0— (the rest was burned, though the comma suggested a five-figure sum)
- M. ... (only the faintest trace of the initial remained)

"It's written on artist paper," Ramsbottom added, slotting it back into the folder. "And the smudges are watercolour paint."

"Do they match the paint you found on Jodie's jacket?"

Ramsbottom nodded. "Any idea what it means?"

Claire narrowed her eyes, seeing the torn note in her mind's eye. "C.H.... L.R.... R.G.... Those are initials. And the figures... debts?"

"Loan shark?" Ramsbottom suggested, his tone hopeful.

Claire shook her head. "I doubt it. Lucy said Jodie was always chasing money, not lending it. And Maria said she had dirt on everyone." She trailed off, piecing it together. "This isn't a loan record—it's a blackmail list."

Ramsbottom's eyes widened. "Interesting."

"Maria said Jodie had something on everyone," she continued. "It's how she kept control. And Lucy said Jodie was desperate for money. What's easier than squeezing it out of people she knows?" She chewed at her lip. "What's Lucy and Jodie's surname?"

"Ross."

"And Ricky's?"

"Greene." His eyes lit up. "Oh. That is rather obvious when you put it like that. But wait." Narrowing his eyes, he seemed to be assessing Claire. "C.H.—Claire Harris? Jodie was blackmailing *you*?"

"No," Claire snapped, rolling her eyes. "I met her for the first time the day before she died. But someone else might have known her well enough to chat over the garden fence."

"Carol Hodgkinson!" Ramsbottom's face lit up, snapping the folder shut. "You and your father share the same brain. You might put me out of a job."

Claire doubted that, but she kept her thoughts to herself. Ramsbottom ran off with his foulder in the direction of the cul-de-sac.

"Hey!" the woman in the burger van cried. "You've forgot your food!"

She held up a hefty bag, which Claire gratefully took as payment for helping Ramsbottom figure out the initials. She almost wanted to run after him, to see what Carol had to say about Jodie blackmailing her for £2000.

But she still needed to talk to Damon.

Inside the empty shop, Damon slouched behind the counter, flipping through a dog-eared comic book. At the sound of the door, he sat up, shoving the comic aside.

"It's fine," Claire said, holding up the bag. "You don't need to look busy if there's nothing to do."

"They used to tell us at the factory there was *always* something to do."

"Lunch is on Ramsbottom," Claire said, setting the bag on the counter—the detective had ordered enough burgers, fries, and all the sides for several people. "And we're not at the factory anymore." She tore open one of the wrappers, the smell of fried onions filling the room. "Though we did spend a lot of years there… side by side… friends… *trusting* each other…"

Damon froze mid-reach for his burger. "Have I done something?" he asked cautiously.

"I'm not sure," Claire replied, watching him closely. "You tell me."

"What have I done?" he whispered. "Claire?"

Claire hated that she had to do this, but she'd promised Sally—and Sally had been right about her ex-husband's wandering eye. Claire didn't want to believe Damon could fit that mould, but ever since she'd found the squatters in her house, nothing in her world had felt the right way up.

"Sally thinks you're acting strange," she blurted out. "She thinks you're being unfaithful."

"What?" Damon choked, his face contorting in shock. "With *who*?"

"She hasn't got that far yet," Claire admitted, guilt twisting her stomach. "Sorry, mate. You're not, are you?"

"*Claire!*" Damon stared at her on the verge of tears, his hurt and anger plain. He turned away, running a hand through his thick hair as he paced behind the counter. "I—I can't believe you'd ask."

"Damon, that's not the refusal I'd hoped for," she said, her voice sharper than she intended. "Mate, I'm sorry, I—"

"No, I'm not."

Damon didn't wait for her to respond. He disappeared into the back, the door clicking shut behind him. Not quite slammed, but firm enough to sting. Another door shutting, one at a time. And this one hurt even more.

"I'm sorry," she called after him, unsure if there was anything she could say to make it right. "I'll leave you alone." She backed away from the counter, hesitating before adding softly, "And I'll leave the food. You know I love you, mate."

And she loved Sally too.

This was exactly what she'd dreaded when she found out two of her closest friends had fallen in love—being piggy in the middle. It had almost been easier back when they couldn't stand to be in the same room.

Leaving Damon to process the accusation, Claire left the shop. She inhaled the crisp air outside, but it did little to steady her nerves.

And the racket coming from behind The Hesketh Arms wasn't helping.

A hammering noise rang out—loud, relentless, and all too familiar after months of builders crawling all over 1 Birch Close.

Ricky's words echoed in her mind.

"Stuart goes where the work is," he'd said.

Weaving through the bustling Christmas market, Claire set off to the pub. If she couldn't fix things with Damon, she could at least try to track down the last suspect on her list.

The sound of hammering echoed from behind The Hesketh Arms as Claire approached. Scaffolding loomed over the canal-side pub, workers of all ages repairing a gutter that had succumbed to the relentless December weather. She scanned the faces, searching for one in particular, but she was disappointed not to see Stuart among them.

Then she spotted him.

He was perched on the canal's edge, his long legs dangling over the side as he ate a thin sandwich, the crusts curling at the edges. Not much of a lunch for a man of his size.

Claire ducked into the pub and bought some packets

of the *Merry Crispmas* mystery crisps. She headed to the canal and sat beside him, the cold stone seeping through her jeans.

Stuart glanced at her, groaned, and took another bite of his sandwich. "What do *you* want?"

"To talk," she said, offering him a packet of crisps.

"And if I don't want to talk?" He eyed the bag before snatching it. "Haven't you got anything better to do?"

"I'm glad you found work," Claire said, ignoring his tone.

"It's a day rate," Stuart replied gruffly. "Just about enough for a night at the B&B. But it's something."

He sounded tired, his shoulders hunched like the weight of the world had settled there.

"You threatened me," Claire said, breaking the silence.

Stuart paused mid-bite. "Did I?"

"That night, outside the house," she pressed. "You said to watch my back."

He shook his head, chewing slowly. "I warned you, that's all. I don't like seeing women wandering around in the dark. Especially not in pyjamas. You're far too trusting."

Claire held his gaze, uncertain whether his words stemmed from protectiveness or condescension. He had a point—she *had* gone straight home afterwards. But the tone he'd used that night had rattled her more than she'd admitted at the time, and he wasn't doing much to endear himself to her now.

"You didn't like Jodie," she said, changing tactics. "What happened between the two of you?"

"What didn't happen?" He gave a hollow chuckle. "That woman was a thorn in everyone's side."

"You threatened to kill her."

He froze, his hand tightening around the crisp packet. It popped, startling them both. The nearby ducks skidded away as crisps sprinkled into the water.

"Who told you that?" he demanded, his tone sharp.

Claire considered confessing it had been Maria, but held back—no sense in revealing all her cards just yet.

"Does it matter?" she asked.

"*I* didn't kill her, if that's what you're thinking." He shovelled in a fistful of crisps, not too taken by the stuffing flavour. Opening his mouth, he let them fall into the canal. "Yeah, I said some things. People do when they're angry."

"What made you so angry?" Claire pressed. "Was it the money?"

"Five hundred bloody quid!" he cried, shaking the rest of the crisps into the canal, which the ducks were grateful for. "She promised to double it, and of course, that was a load of rubbish. I thought she had some scheme or something. She talked the talk, but there was nothing behind it. I still don't know what she did with it."

"I heard she gambled it away on the horses."

"Seriously?" Stuart whipped his head to glare at her. "I was never getting it back, was I?"

Claire smiled an apology. "Doesn't seem that way."

"She always acted so much better than us all," he continued, dropping to a dark whisper. "A total fraud. I don't know why that sister of hers went along with everything. You couldn't get between them. Except for…"

Stuart didn't finish his sentence, but Claire had a feeling of where he'd been going.

"Except for Ricky?"

"Dumb kid," Stuart said, and Claire took that as confirmation. "Seemed to think love could save the day. And seemed to think Jodie would let him get away with taking Lucy away."

"He tried to take her?"

"Metaphorically, I mean," he said, stumbling over the word. "Jodie didn't want anything coming between her and Lucy. Have you seen Lucy's work?"

"Not yet."

"Well, she's grand. Far better than what Jodie had her doing."

Claire leaned in. "And what did Jodie have her doing?"

"That's for Lucy to tell you, isn't it?" he grunted. "All I cared about was getting my money back. I didn't care how. I was never supposed to be with them all for that long. Jodie made out like we'd all be rich one day, and I guess it's true what they say. A sucker is born every minute, and it was me."

"Is that why you threatened her?" Claire pushed. "The night before she died?"

"It was an empty threat," he said, growing tired with the questions. "I told her she'd better pay me by sunrise." His voice dropped, his temper simmering beneath the surface. "But I didn't bloody kill her. I wanted my money, not a murder charge. I'd told her that before and never followed through. I just wanted to *scare* her, is all."

"And did it?"

He laughed. "What do you think? Jodie was a law unto herself. Nothing phased her. Just hearing that she was a gambler has shocked me. If I'd known, I could have used that against her."

"Blackmail, you mean?"

"So what?" he cried, defensive. "Jodie had a way of getting under people's skin, alright? She was always squirrelling information away. If she knew something about you, she'd use it. Blackmail, threats… the lot. I wasn't the only one who wanted her gone."

"And what dirt did she have on you?"

Stuart scowled, his tough exterior cracking as he glanced back at the scaffolding.

"Just stuff from before," he said. "She went digging online—found old reviews. Cowboy builder stuff that I'm not proud of. She threatened to make sure everyone knew. And that they would always know. She made out like there was no escaping her." As though hearing the insinuation, he added, "But like I keep telling you, I didn't kill her."

Claire studied him. "Why did you join the squatters?"

His gaze flicked to the canal. "Where else was I supposed to go? I lost my building business when someone stole my van. I couldn't replace it—no savings. I tried to make it work with contract work like this but it didn't stop me from being evicted. I was in Starfall Park one day and I saw this young girl with purple hair painting Starfall House. I didn't want anything from her, mind you," he added quickly. "I just wanted to watch. I'd never seen anything like it. It was like she was photographing what she could see with her brush, only better. We got talking and she told me it was her favourite place, and next thing I know, I'd moved in with her, Ricky, and Maria. Jodie came after."

"She took over, didn't she?"

"And stole from Maria!" he cried, shaking his head at the water as the ducks drifted away after their fill of crisps. "Jodie made out like any of us could be out of the group if she said so. I could tell she never liked me, but when she found out I had that money, she had a use for me."

"So, you hated her, and she hated you."

"Sounds about right," Stuart said bitterly. "But hate doesn't mean murder."

"Where were you when Jodie died?"

"I was asleep. Same as everyone else."

"Alone?"

He nodded. "I would have been with Ricky, but Jodie kicked him out, and I have no idea where he stayed. So, no—nobody can back up my story. But that's where I was. I'm a heavy sleeper. When you're in the trade, you learn to get your head down when you can. The first I heard about what happened was when the police dragged me down, and you saw that."

"I did," Claire agreed. "But you could have snuck down and gone back to bed."

"Yeah? If that's what you think, any of us could." Stuart moved closer, his expression dark. "You think you've got me figured out, don't you? Yeah, I'm angry. Yeah, I wanted my money. But I *didn't* kill her." He jabbed a finger towards her. "You want answers? Look at the others. Ricky, Lucy, even Maria. They all had reasons to want Jodie gone."

"And Carol Hodgkinson?"

Stuart blinked, caught off guard. "The neighbour? What's she got to do with this?"

"She was seen talking to someone over the garden fence about an hour before Jodie died, and I've just learned that Jodie might have been blackmailing Carol too." She paused, but he offered no reaction—just like when he'd first seen Jodie's body in the kitchen. "Know anything about that?"

"Why would I?" Stuart stood abruptly, towering over her. "I'm done talking. Watch your back, Claire. I mean it this time." He scooped up a brown paper bag she hadn't noticed, a familiar bottle of whisky poking out the top—her dad drank the same one. "Don't look at me like that, alright?" he barked. "It was a gift."

As Stuart stalked off, Claire stayed seated by the canal, the winter wind tugging at her hair. He had painted a clear picture of his anger and motives, but was that enough to make him a killer?

She wasn't sure he was her prime suspect anymore, but the more she heard about Lucy and her art, the more questions she had. If Lucy had once told Stuart that Starfall Park was her favourite spot, it seemed as good a place as any to start looking for the girl with the purple hair.

AS SHE APPROACHED THE LOCALLY FAMOUS STARFALL Park's wrought-iron gates next to The Park Inn pub, the faint strum of a guitar reached her ears. The sound wasn't unpleasant, but it was far from polished—hesitant and rough around the edges, as though the player was still finding their rhythm.

Ricky sat cross-legged near the park's entrance, a battered hat on the ground beside him, scattered with loose coins. The guitar he held wasn't the old acoustic model she'd seen him cradling in the house. This one was newer, sleeker, and he didn't quite seem sure of how to use it.

Claire slowed, watching him from a distance. His hunched shoulders and bowed head painted a picture of a man trying to fade into the background. Yet his restless eyes darted around, scanning for passersby who might toss a coin or two.

"Morning," Claire said casually as she approached.

Ricky's fingers halted on the strings, his head snapping like a startled rabbit. "Claire," he muttered, his voice tight. He shifted uncomfortably, his eyes darting away. "Didn't expect to see you."

"I fancied a Sunday stroll around my favourite park," she replied, nodding towards the hat. "Is that to pay my gran's lodging fee?"

Ricky brushed a strand of greasy hair from his face. "Just trying to make ends meet. You know how it is."

She didn't, not like this, at least. She'd had hard times, but she'd never had to put a hat out in the street.

"Aren't you cold?" she asked.

"You get used to it."

She shrugged off her jacket and held it out. He considered the offer for a moment before grabbing it. He draped it over his shoulders, far too big for him, but he seemed warmer. Claire was fine in her jumper, for now.

"Still no news on your other guitar?" she asked.

"Nope," he said quickly. His fingers plucked at the strings, more for something to do than to play. "Stop asking. I already told you I left it at the house."

Claire tilted her head, studying him. His movements were jittery, his knee bouncing like he couldn't sit still. There was a nervous energy about him, an edge of desperation that seemed to hum beneath the surface.

"You know one of the strings was wrapped around Jodie's hand?" she said.

"Among other things," he replied with a shrug. "Paint, a hammer, and some of Maria's thread."

"I didn't hear about the thread."

"Maybe you're not as in the loop as you thought," he said, still strumming. "If you're not going to throw me some coins, clear off. You're scaring away the punters."

But as Claire glanced around, she noticed there weren't many people out on this cold Sunday, even with Christmas just around the corner. She reached into her pocket, pulled out a crisp blue five-pound note, and tossed it into Ricky's hat.

"You're pretty good," she offered. "Used to play in a band, right?"

Ricky's face twitched. "Yep. Lead guitarist. We used to pack out pubs and even played a festival once. But it's all politics, you know? Everyone wants to follow the crowd. No one cares about the art."

"Is that why they kicked you out?"

Ricky's fingers stilled again, his jaw tightening. "They didn't *kick* me out. *I* left. Couldn't stand their sellout crap. You wouldn't understand. It's hard being the one who *actually* cares. The one who sees things differently."

Claire bit back a response. His words sounded rehearsed, like something he'd told himself a thousand times to stave off the truth. But before she could push further, a voice rang out from the other side of the park gate.

"Hey! That's *my* guitar!"

Both Claire and Ricky turned as a young man in a puffer jacket stormed towards them, pointing an accusatory finger. Ricky's face went pale, his eyes darting to the approaching man and then to Claire. For a heartbeat, he seemed frozen, like a deer caught in headlights.

"I left it at the bus stop for less than a minute," the man cried, "and now here you are, playing it like it's yours! *Thief!*"

Then, without a word, he grabbed his hat and bolted, leaving the guitar and Claire's coat behind.

"*Oi!*" the man shouted, but Ricky was already

disappearing up the lane, his gangly frame weaving between the parked cars. "If you see him again, call the police."

Claire nodded absently, her thoughts elsewhere as she climbed back into her coat. She couldn't shake the image of Ricky's panicked face, the way he'd run at the first sign of confrontation. He wasn't just down on his luck—he was drowning in it. And worse, he was staying in her gran's house.

Trying to gather her thoughts, Claire walked a lap of Starfall Park, but there was no sign of purple-haired Lucy.

On her way to warn her gran about her new lodger's sticky fingers, Claire followed a plume of cigarette smoke drifting near the mechanic's garage at the end of the street. She hadn't planned to stop, but the sight of Stuart leaning against the wall, his phone pressed to his ear, froze her in place.

He spoke fast, his words tumbling out in fits and bursts, struggling to get a word in while someone ranted at him on the other end. She couldn't make out much, but his agitation was unmistakable. His free hand jabbed the air with every other word, the cigarette dangling precariously between his fingers.

"No, *you* listen to *me*," he hissed. "I've got nothing left to give, so we're going to do this the other way now. *You* owe *me*. Got it? I know *everything*."

Claire ducked into the shadow of the gallery, straining her ears to listen.

"I told you, it's not *my* problem anymore!" Stuart barked, throwing his hands up. "You're on your own. I never agreed to cover for you, I—"

He spun around, catching Claire's efforts to blend into the walls as the afternoon light faded. It wasn't dark enough that it might have worked, but she hadn't known what else to do. He hung up and seemed unsure of what to do with himself.

"You know, don't you?" she said, stepping into the glow as the street lights hummed to life. "*You* know who killed Jodie."

"I've already told you—"

"To watch my back," Claire interrupted, narrowing her eyes. How much of what he'd said to her by the canal had been true? Straightening her shoulders, she said, "From the sounds of that phone call, mate, it's *your* back you should be worrying about."

Stuart scoffed, shaking his head. "You don't get it, do you? Knowing things around here doesn't keep you safe —it paints a target on your back."

"That's not an answer," she pressed, her voice cutting

through the rising hum of the streetlights flickering to life. "You *know*."

"It's the only answer you're getting," he muttered, shoving his phone into his pocket. He brushed past her and said, "Go home, Claire. Forget you saw me. Forget all of this."

Claire watched as he disappeared down the street, his heavy footsteps fading into the distance. Her heart pounded, frustration simmering in her chest.

He knew something important, but getting it out of him would take more than a packet of crisps and a confrontation on the street. As the wind picked up, she turned towards Greta's cottage. The image of Stuart's agitated phone call burned into her mind.

Secrets like Stuart's didn't stay hidden for long in a village like this. Claire would make sure of it—and she was willing to dig even deeper to find out what he was hiding.

CHAPTER TEN

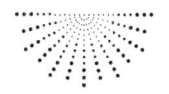

Claire approached the candle shop, hoping to see Damon calm and collected through the window, but the darkness inside told another story. A note flapped against the glass: *Closed due to unforeseen circumstances.* The handwriting was sloppy, the kind Damon used when his head was elsewhere.

She pulled the note down, the paper crinkling in her hand. The unforeseen circumstances were that she'd ambushed him without thinking things through. She sighed, letting herself into the empty shop.

She perched on a stool behind the counter, her eyes wandering the shelves without seeing them. She hadn't meant to push Damon away, but juggling everything—Damon, Sally, the murder investigation, the squatters—

had left her stretched thin. If things had been different, maybe she would've approached him better.

Her thoughts turned to Stuart. He knew more than he was saying, she was sure of it. But how could she get him to trust her? To believe that it was safe to tell her the truth?

She pulled out her phone, staring at the screen for a moment.

CLAIRE

I'm sorry. Are you at home?

DAMON

No

One word, flat and cold. *No* to being home, or *no* to the apology? Maybe both. She blinked at the screen, her stomach sinking. Damon didn't want to talk—at least not to her. Sally might have been right about him acting differently, but after the way she'd confronted him earlier, could she really blame him for keeping his distance?

She glanced around the dark shop one more time, the shelves lined with her carefully crafted work. This was supposed to be her safe place, her sanctuary. But tonight, it felt as empty as she did.

With a deep breath, she locked the door behind her. It was time to go home. Time to stop chasing answers she wasn't ready for.

"Four down, 'Seasonal gift bearer,'" Alan called out. "Ten letters."

"Father Christmas," Janet answered, holding a stubborn corner of wrapping paper with a mug.

"That's not ten letters," Alan said, pencil hovering.

Claire sighed, turning away from the window. "Santa Claus."

"Ah! Good thinking, little one."

But even with the calm of her parents' house, Claire couldn't sit still. The events of the past few days were mulling, her thoughts a bubbling brew. She slipped into her coat and boots, craving the fresh air.

The cul-de-sac was lively, the kids attaching a crooked carrot nose to their snowman. They were playing with the two Chopra children, boys around the same ages as Amelia and Hugo. Claire would go across and introduce herself properly once they'd settled in.

Across the way, Carol Hodgkinson stood at her gate, tossing something else into her wheelie bin. Claire hesitated, debating whether to approach and clear up the blackmail note. But before she could decide, Carol's gaze landed on her, sharp and unyielding.

"*You*," Carol hissed. "It's you, isn't it? Trying to get under my skin. Trying to drive me crazy!"

Claire blinked, startled. "I have no idea what you're talking about."

"Don't play dumb with me." Carol's breath puffed furiously in the cold as she jabbed a gloved finger towards Claire. "You think I don't know what you're up to? Snooping around, asking questions. You think you're so clever, don't you?"

"Carol," Claire said, keeping her tone even, "I'm just trying to figure out what happened. This isn't only about you."

"Oh, but it *is*," Carol snapped, her voice rising. "Everything is about me now, isn't it? That's what you want. To see me *humiliated*?"

Claire tilted her head, watching Carol with a mix of confusion and suspicion. "If this has anything to do with Jodie blackmailing you, then you're the one making it about you."

The colour drained from Carol's face. Her lips parted, then snapped shut again. "How do you—" She stopped herself, her eyes narrowing.

Claire seized the opening. "You were talking to her over the fence. Early morning—around five, yesterday. You knew her before she came here, didn't you?"

Silence. Carol's face twisted, but no words came. She fumbled with something in her pocket, pulled it out, and shoved it into her wheelie bin with more force than necessary.

Another slammed door, and Carol vanished. Claire waited, expecting the familiar twitch of the curtain. But nothing came. The house remained dark and silent.

Her curiosity now piqued, Claire walked to the bin. She hesitated for only a second before lifting the lid. On top of the discarded pinecone wreath lay a screwed-up ball of paper. She carefully pulled it out, smoothing it against her knee.

Double, or I tell. Usual place. TONIGHT.

Her stomach dropped. The handwriting was hurried, but the meaning was clear: blackmail.

Carol Hodgkinson had just risen to the top of her list of suspects.

CLAIRE PACED IN THE DINING ROOM ALONE, THE CRUMPLED blackmail note spread flat on the table before her.

Double what?

The two thousand pounds she'd seen written on the list Ramsbottom had shown her earlier?

And where was the usual place?

Her fingers hovered over her phone, the urge to call Ramsbottom tugging at her. But she hesitated. What would she even say? That Carol Hodgkinson had tossed a note into the bin that might link her to Jodie's death? That she *felt* like Carol was hiding something?

It wasn't enough. Ramsbottom wouldn't take her neighbour seriously as a suspect, not without something concrete—especially if he'd already spoken to Carol about her initials appearing on the note.

And then there was Stuart.

Someone had been trying to blackmail him too. Jodie's murderer, if Claire's hunch was right. She replayed his phone call in her mind: he'd said he was going to turn the tables, play by his rules.

Were Carol and Stuart blackmailing each other?

She sighed and sank into a chair, her forehead resting against the cold, polished wood of the dining room table. The sharp scent of furniture polish hit her nose, turning her stomach.

If Carol was involved in this—if she planned to meet someone to pay them off—then Claire needed to know when and where. She'd been accused of being nosy plenty of times before, but tonight, she'd lean into it.

"Curtain twitching it is," she said grimly, folding up the note and venturing off into the house for a better view of Birch Close.

SPICED ORANGE SUSPICION

WHILE *HOME ALONE 2* PLAYED IN THE BACKGROUND, Claire perched by the front window, her gaze fixed on the cul-de-sac as fresh snow fluttered. The kids' laughter rang out every few minutes, punctuating the slapstick antics on screen. She tried to focus, but her eyes drifted back to the glow of Carol's house.

One by one, the lights clicked off—Carol was heading out.

"I'm craving chocolate," Claire announced, letting the curtain fall. "Does anyone else want anything from the shop?"

"Oh, Claire!" Janet groaned from her spot on the sofa, surrounded by a fortress of cushions. "*Really?*"

"Sweets!" Amelia piped up from the floor, her eyes glued to the screen.

"Sweets," Hugo echoed over his console.

"Sweets *and* chocolate," Alan added without looking up from his crossword.

"Sweets," Ryan called from the kitchen where he'd been painting.

Janet sighed dramatically. "Well, I'm not going to be left out, am I? A *small* bar of chocolate. And not the cheap stuff!"

Claire hurried into the hallway, pulling on her dad's oversized coat. She looped her mother's scarf around her neck, tugged Ryan's knitted hat low over her ears, and crammed the kids' gloves onto her hands. Bundled up in a mishmash of borrowed clothing, she caught her reflection in the mirror by the door. She looked like a walking lost-and-found box and nothing like herself.

"Back soon!" she called, tucking her hair into the hat.

Claire stepped into the snow, her mother's boots compressing the fluffy snow. As she'd predicted, it didn't take long for Carol to emerge, pulling her coat tight against the cold. She ignored the car parked in her driveway and set off on foot down the lane.

Claire lingered, giving Carol a headstart before following. She kept her steps light, the only sounds in the still night the faint crunch of their boots on snow. She wished she'd brought Spud along—a dog would make her presence less suspicious. Then again, Spud's erratic behaviour wouldn't help her keep a low profile.

Carol never looked back. Not once. Claire's chest tightened. Whatever Carol was heading towards, it must have been more frightening than anything behind her.

The soft glow of the village lights came into view, and Claire's resolve sharpened. She had to know what Carol was hiding. Whatever it was, it might be the key to making sense of everything.

Keeping her pace steady, Claire followed Carol into the village. She had no idea who Carol was about to meet —or what she'd find waiting for her.

Carol moved quickly, weaving through the streets before slipping down the back alley behind Claire's row of shops. Claire followed, keeping to the shadows. They emerged near the post office, where Carol cut a diagonal line across the roundabout, heading for The Park Inn.

The Park Inn wasn't just any pub—it was the village's 'other' pub. To tourists, it was quaint and picturesque and at the foot of Starfall Park, a place that might pop up in a glossy travel brochures. To locals, it was the 'secrets pub' where stolen glances and whispered conversations meant more than the beer. Affairs and dodgy dealings, or so Claire was always hearing. She knew the food was good these days since Grant took over last Christmas, but whatever Carol was there for, Claire doubted it was dinner.

She glanced down at her mismatched outfit, her borrowed coat and scarf swallowing her whole. She looked far too bundled up to blend in, and if she unravelled inside, she'd reveal herself.

She lingered outside, pulling out her phone as cover. With her head down, she edged closer to the window, steamed up with condensation. A glance inside revealed Stuart at the bar, his shoulders hunched as he nursed a drink. Was he waiting for Carol?

Claire's gaze shifted to a booth partially hidden in the corner. Carol sat alone, her head darting in every direction like a skittish bird. She checked her watch, her gaze dancing nervously around the place before she pulled out a thick envelope. She peeked inside. Claire couldn't be sure, but it seemed to be stuffed with cash.

Carol *was* being blackmailed by someone new.

But by who? And why?

The question hung in the air as Claire turned away from the window, her mind racing. She was startled by the sharp crunch of footsteps on the pavement, followed by a familiar voice laced with irritation.

"You're *unbelievable*, you know that?"

Claire spun to see Maria approaching, her eyes blazing.

"What?" Claire asked, feigning innocence.

"Following people. Snooping around." Maria jabbed a finger at her. "And *we're* the criminals, apparently."

"Why are you so defensive, Maria?" Claire replied. "What do you know?"

"You learn to be defensive. It's a way of life. Survival of the fittest."

"And was Jodie not one of the fittest?" Claire pressed, her voice low. "Is that why she died?"

Maria's expression darkened, her gaze narrowing into sharp slits. For a moment, the pressure crackled between them like static electricity.

"How should I know?" Maria muttered.

Her defensiveness didn't just feel hostile—it felt rehearsed, like a shield she'd been holding up for years.

Lucy and Ricky appeared next, walking side by side. Lucy looked hesitant, her arms wrapped around herself, while Ricky strode confidently as though he hadn't run for his life after stealing a guitar earlier.

They passed Claire, heading into the pub without a word. Claire stared after them, her thoughts tangled. Everyone was there now: Stuart, Carol, Maria, Lucy, Ricky.

Then, from the direction of the square came the distinctive sound of an argument growing closer—loud, heated, and unmistakably Sally.

"I can't do this, Damon!" Sally's voice rang out, and Claire's heart sank.

Sally emerged near the post office, her hands flying up in exasperation. Damon trailed behind her, his face flushed as he tried to keep up.

"Sally, *please*," Damon called, his voice cracking. "Let me *explain*."

Sally spun around. "Explain *what*? The secrecy? The sneaking around? It's *gaslighting*, Damon!"

"I'm not gaslighting you!" he pleaded. "You just think I am."

"That's what a gaslighter *would* say!" Sally roared, her eyes blazing. Without waiting for a response, she ran through the side entrance of Starfall Park, heading up the hill to her house, missing Claire in her disguise.

Claire tugged her hat off. Damon noticed her, and his

face flushed an even deeper red. He reached into his pocket as he approached her, his hands trembling.

"How could I tell her?" he said, his voice low and tight. "It was supposed to be a surprise for Christmas. But apparently, I'm not good at planning surprises. I'm an idiot, Claire."

"I don't think she's good at receiving them. Her ex-husband was full of surprises."

"I *am* an idiot. I didn't think of that. All those years I spent being single, thinking I was better off, and now I have someone like Sally, and I'm screwing it all up because I don't know how to do any of this stuff."

"What stuff, Damon?"

He dug in his pocket and pulled out a small leather box with gold detailing. Claire's heart skipped a beat as he snapped it open. Inside was a diamond ring, simple but stunning, catching a twinkle from the lights outside the pub.

"*This* why I wanted your help," Damon whispered as his teary eyes searched Claire's. "But then I thought if I told you, you might tell Sally, and—"

"Oh, Damon," Claire said, wrapping him in a tight hug. "I'll talk to Sally. We'll sort this out. She loves you. You know she does—"

A commotion erupted from inside the pub, cutting her off. There was a loud thud, followed by gasps and shouts. Damon snapped the box shut and pocketed it.

"What now?" she muttered.

Through the window, Claire saw Stuart lying sprawled on the floor, his body convulsing, his stool knocked over. Maria knelt at his side, her hands shaking as she tried to steady him.

"What's wrong?" Maria cried. "Stuart? What's happening?"

Lucy clung to Ricky's chest, her face buried. Ricky looked on with a confused twist in his brows, his hand hovering protectively over Lucy. Without Jodie, it seemed they had nothing to hide.

At the bar, Carol stood frozen, her jaw slack. The envelope poked out of her pocket, but she didn't seem to notice. She watched Stuart's writhing form on the floor, and without a word, she turned and bolted, shoving past Claire on her way out.

"*Carol*!" Claire called after her, but the woman didn't stop.

The envelope tumbled from Carol's pocket as she fled. It hit the pavement, and the wind picked it up, scattering colourful pound notes across the street.

Claire dove to grab them, Damon joining her. His eyes widened as he picked up a handful.

"There's *thousands* here," he whispered. "What's going on?"

Inside the pub, the shouts grew louder, and then, silence. With fistfuls of Carol's cash, Claire returned to the window in time to see Maria straightening up, shaking her head.

"What happened to him?" Lucy asked.

"Heart attack or something?" Ricky suggested. "He was a drinker."

"He's dead," Maria announced in a flat voice that carried around the quiet pub. "Stuart's dead."

Claire froze, the weight of the blackmail money burning in her hands. Her chest tightened as she looked at Damon, who met her gaze with wide, uncertain eyes. The confusion mirrored between them only deepened the knot in her stomach.

She turned back to the pub, where the faint murmur of voices had given way to a chilling silence. Another death. Another life cut short.

And once again, the same people had all been present.

LATER THAT NIGHT, CLAIRE LAY CURLED UP IN BED, RYAN'S arm draped around her. His steady breathing should have been a comfort, but her thoughts churned too violently to let her rest.

"He *knew*, Ryan," she whispered, her voice trembling. "Stuart knew who killed Jodie. That person was blackmailing him, and then he tried to turn the tables to blackmail them back. And Carol shows up at the pub with an envelope of cash, and suddenly Stuart is dead."

Ryan's hand tightened on her waist, his breath warm against her neck. "It could have been natural causes," he murmured, though even he didn't sound convinced.

"But we *know* it wasn't," she said firmly. "It's happened again, Ryan. Another death and I couldn't stop it. I talked to Stuart this afternoon. I bought him crisps." Her voice broke as she added, "Looking back, he might have been the most honest person with me so far."

Ryan shifted, propping himself up on one elbow. "Except he didn't tell you what he *really* knew," he pointed out as the cats scattered from the sudden movement. "You had to overhear that."

"He was scared," Claire said, flicking off the bedside lamp. The darkness pressed in, but it didn't feel restful. "And it seems he had good reason to be."

Ryan pulled her closer, his silence more reassuring than any words could be. Claire stared into the shadows, replaying every word, every look, every unanswered question. Stuart had been scared, yes—but of who?

And how many more people would pay the price before she figured it out?

CHAPTER ELEVEN

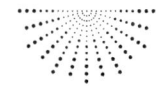

"It wasn't a heart attack," Ramsbottom announced in the quiet candle shop the next morning. "Stuart was poisoned with a large quantity of…" He paused, squinting at his notes, "… *Toluene?*"

Janet wrinkled her nose. "Never heard of it."

"Toluene," Ramsbottom repeated with more confidence. "It's a solvent, found in all sorts of things—nail varnish remover, adhesives." He gestured around the shop. "Candles."

Claire's stomach tightened. "Not *my* candles. I think we used it back at the factory, but I don't use chemicals like that."

"I didn't say you did," he replied with a chuckle. "But it's worth asking—do you stock anything with it?"

"No," Claire said. "I don't think so, but you're welcome to check."

"I'll take your word for it," Ramsbottom said, jotting something in his notebook. "Wherever this stuff came from, Stuart ingested a fatal dose. This wasn't some accidental exposure, and I doubt he took it voluntarily. Someone wanted him dead."

The words settled uneasily in the room, and Claire was glad there were only a few customers too busy shopping to be paying attention. She'd given Damon the day off.

"Wouldn't he have tasted it?" Alan suggested, fiddling with the samples on the counter. "To kill a man like that, surely it would take an enormous quantity."

"The bar staff said he'd been there for hours drinking straight whisky," Ramsbottom confirmed. "According to them, he kept asking for the time. He gave them the impression he was waiting for someone."

"Carol?" Claire suggested. "She was convinced I'd sent her the blackmail note before I noticed her at The Park Inn." She hadn't told anyone she'd followed Carol. "I think she thought I was messing with her."

"Ah, yes." Ramsbottom turned back a page, scratching his toupee with the tip of his pen. "She claims she was there to 'get out of the house,' and there was nothing untoward going on."

"More lies," Janet said, pursing her lips. "I wouldn't be

surprised if she was behind this. She killed Jodie because she was blackmailing her, and then killed Stuart because he took over the blackmailing."

"We don't know it was Stuart who blackmailed Carol," Claire said.

"You just insinuated it, dear," Janet protested.

"The rest of the group were there too," Claire pointed out in a more measured tone. "Any one of them could have sent Carol that note."

"Exactly, little one," her father said, sending her a wink of support. "The same way any of them could have poisoned Stuart. Best to keep all options open."

"Yes, but it was likely Stuart, right?" Janet searched between the DI and the retired DI, but neither co-signed her theory. "He's proved himself to be a sketchy fella after being arrested for vandalising his old employers' building site. And he was *heard* threatening Jodie's life."

"A moment ago, you thought Carol killed Jodie," Claire reminded her.

"And I can still imagine she did. But what *if* Stuart killed Jodie to take over her little blackmailing empire, and then Carol killed him because she's Carol Hodgkinson—you don't need more of a reason than that." Janet spread her hands out, but still, nobody agreed. "You'll see I'm right when the dirty laundry is hung out to dry."

Claire's throat tightened. She thought of the cash

envelope sitting in her bag in the storeroom—she hadn't told them about the money either.

"She had an envelope with her," she revealed. "It looked like money."

"Did you see an exchange, little one?"

"No." Claire hesitated, fingers curling around the edge of the counter. "She dropped the envelope when she ran out. Some of it blew away."

"Serves her right," Janet muttered, checking her nails. "Imagine what she must have done that she was able to be blackmailed for thousands. It's not like any of us have been on the receiving end of that, and for good reason. We're upstanding citizens!"

"As is Carol," Alan said firmly. "I know you've always clashed with her, dear, but there is such a thing as a bias."

"Sometimes biases are correct," Janet said under her breath, but she didn't take it further. Turning to Ramsbottom, she asked, "What about the rest of that list? The initials?"

Ramsbottom flipped open his notebook again, running a finger down the page. "C.H., L.R., R.G., and a faint M. The figures beside them suggest payments—some settled, some outstanding."

"Carol, Lucy, Ricky," Claire said softly. "And Maria."

"All except Stuart?" Alan said.

"Because Stuart wasn't being blackmailed by Jodie,"

Claire pointed out. "Stuart was the one being owed money. Lucy said Jodie lost it on horse racing."

"I've had to escort Jodie out of the bookies a few times," Ramsbottom admitted, his tone grim. "She'd lose all her money, and then she'd start harassing other people for loans. She was always convinced she'd get it to them. I think even she believed it."

Alan hummed some agreement. "Perhaps she saw the blackmailing as a more sure-fire gamble. Bigger risks, but much bigger rewards, if we're to assume Carol already paid Jodie £2000."

"Carol's secret must be *shocking*," Janet said, relishing the thought too much. "I can't wait to hear it."

"I'll be paying her a visit," Ramsbottom said, snapping his pad shut before tucking it away. "And I suggest you lot keep your noses clean. I don't want any more surprises after last night. This case was already giving me a headache." He sighed. "Oh, how I was looking forward to Christmas!"

"Crime doesn't stop for Christmas, old friend," Alan said. "It's only the most wonderful time of year for some."

With that, DI Ramsbottom tipped his head and strode out, leaving a heavy silence in his wake.

Claire exhaled, her hands trembling. Janet busied herself tidying a stack of candles, muttering under her breath about the audacity of it all. Alan stepped closer, his voice low.

"Are you alright, little one?"

Claire nodded, though she didn't feel it. "I just want this to be over before someone else gets hurt."

"It will be." He squeezed her shoulder. "Did you notice the final sum on the page? The one that was ripped off?"

"Next to Ricky's name?"

He nodded. "Judging by where Jodie put that comma, it sounds like Carol got off lightly with a £2000 sum when Jodie wanted £10,000 from Ricky." Leaning in, he whispered, "Five times more money for five times the consequences? So, the question is…"

Picking up the sentence, Claire said, "… What did Ricky do that was bad enough for Jodie to think she could extract that much money from Ricky?"

"Just something to think about," he said, spreading his hands across the counter as he stood behind the till. "That's what I'd be interested in finding out. I'll watch things here."

Claire would—and Ricky was still lodging with Granny Greta as of that morning. She'd speak to him again, but first, she had two priorities: confront Carol with what was left of the £4000 she and Damon had salvaged from the wind, and have lunch with Ryan.

Claire met Ryan by the clock tower, its iron hands marking the steady creep toward noon. The Christmas market had calmed after the morning rush.

"Where do you fancy?" she asked, rubbing her hands together before shivering set in. "I could eat a small horse."

"How about a packed lunch?" Ryan gave her a small smile and patted the canvas bag slung over his shoulder. "I thought we could do something different."

Claire raised an eyebrow. "Different?"

"You'll see." He motioned for her to follow, leading her past the stalls and down the quiet side street.

They walked past Marley's Café, the Still Loved second-hand clothes shop, and straight into the small Northash Gallery.

Inside, the hum of the heaters welcomed them. Ryan guided her to the far end of the gallery, stopping in front of a painting of Northash's rolling hills under a vibrant sunset.

They stood there, unwrapping sausage rolls from greaseproof paper and sipping juice from cartons pilfered from the kids' school dinner supplies. Claire couldn't help but laugh at the absurdity of it, but Ryan's expression was serious.

"What do you think?" he asked, gesturing to the painting.

"It's lovely," Claire said, chewing thoughtfully. "I like the colours. It's one of Susan Bello Sa'ad's pieces, isn't it?"

Ryan nodded. "Yeah. But here's the thing—Susan Bello Sa'ad is dead."

Claire blinked at him. "Okay?"

"She's dead," he repeated, leaning closer to the painting, "and this painting *cannot* exist."

"Why not?"

"Because it was sold six months ago," Ryan said, pulling out his phone. He swiped to a social media post showing the same painting hanging in someone's study. "Here it is, in a private collection."

"Maybe they sold it back to the gallery?"

"Possibly," Ryan said, his tone unconvinced. "But look at this one." He moved to another painting, this time an abstract geometric piece with bold, chaotic colours that seemed to clash and harmonise all at once. "This artist's tagged pictures show three versions of this painting."

"Could he have painted three?"

Ryan shook his head. "In his bio, he says he only paints originals. No commissions, no duplicates."

He stepped to another painting, this one more familiar.

"Starfall Observatory," she said. "Didn't you sell this one already?"

The painting depicted the iconic structure atop the hill in the park, bathed in golden autumn light. She remembered that day vividly—the crispy leaves, the way Ryan had sketched out the composition while she sipped too-hot coffee, keeping Amelia and Hugo occupied on the swings.

"What do you see?" he asked.

"One of my favourites of yours," Claire said, a smile tugging at her lips. "I love how you captured that yellow light you only get that time of year."

"Hmm." Ryan sighed. "It's not *my* painting, Claire."

"It is," she insisted. "I watched you paint it."

"This isn't mine. I mean, it *is* mine, but it's not. This one is better. The details, the brushstrokes… it's not my work."

Claire brushed her fingers across the canvas. The texture felt real—it wasn't a print.

"Are you sure?" she asked.

"I'm sure." Ryan nodded. "Whoever painted this, they improved it. I received the money, but the receipt of who bought the original was scrubbed from the records."

Claire took a step back, scanning the gallery with fresh eyes.

"These are Lucy's paintings, aren't they?"

"Remember what Picasso said? 'Good artists copy, great artists steal.'" He let out a low, almost impressed sigh as his eyes lingered on the art. "And incredible artists, they forge."

"If you weren't so sure, I'd never have known," she

said. "These are incredible. It's not just mimicry. It's like she sees."

"She sees?"

"Something Ricky said. Lucy *saw*."

"You think Jodie put her up to this?"

"She must have?" Claire said, unsure of any other explanation. "Lucy said Jodie faked her CV to get the job, and Ricky said Jodie got her fired. 'Grassed' on her. But why copy when she can paint like this? *Her* work should be lining a gallery."

"Her paintings *are* lining a gallery." Ryan gestured to the walls around them. "This gallery. And the owner has no idea how many are fakes and how many are originals. He's been bringing artists in to assess their work, and half of them can't tell." Leaning closer, he added, "There's a ten percent commission for every piece sold. Mine don't go for much, but some of these pieces rack up."

"This was her project," Claire thought aloud. "I overheard Lucy and Maria talking about it, but like everything else, Lucy didn't want to go into it."

"But why would Jodie expose her sister if they made money from it?" Ryan asked. "Like I said, the owner never noticed. Someone told him."

Claire tilted her head, studying the painting of Starfall Observatory again. "Because Jodie could? Because she had to keep control. And because…" She hesitated, the thought sinking in. "… because she didn't want to share."

Ryan looked at her, his brow furrowed. "Share what?"

"Her talent. Her money. Her independence?" Claire suggested, her voice tightening. "Jodie saw her as a meal ticket. But maybe this gave Lucy the confidence to stand up for herself?"

"And Jodie made sure she couldn't," Ryan finished. "That's so sad. Lucy hasn't only copied—she's mastered style after style. It's one thing to be able to paint a landscape, but she can paint anything. She's a *savant*."

While Ryan tried to extract more details from the owner in the office, he left Claire alone with her thoughts. The quiet of the gallery, punctuated only by the distant droning of someone conducting a small tour, was almost soothing—until she spotted Maria.

Maria stood near the entrance, looking out of place in her dark layers. Her jacket was damp from the cold, her scarf pulled tight, and her eyes darted around as though she knew she was out of place. She noticed Claire and exhaled.

"*You* again," Maria said, her voice low but direct.

Claire walked over, hoping this was her moment to talk to Maria alone. She noticed Maria's gaze shift to the floor, her lips pressing into a thin line as if she were wrestling with herself. Her defensive edge softened for a moment, revealing a hint of vulnerability that caught Claire off guard. Was she about to let her guard down?

"I wasn't looking for you," Claire said. "I promise."

"No, but I've been hoping to see you." Maria glanced over her shoulder as though checking for eavesdroppers, then motioned for them to move closer to the wall. "I don't know what your game is, but you keep popping up everywhere knowing everyone's business, and it's only a matter of time before you start digging into me and my life, and I don't want you to waste your time."

The directness of Maria's words took Claire aback. She'd wanted to talk to Maria from the beginning, but now Maria had sought her out, offering information unprompted before Claire even had the chance to ask. Suspicion prickled at the edges of her thoughts.

She pictured both crime scenes—both times, Maria had been the first to rush to the victims' sides despite her apparent lack of affection for Jodie or Stuart.

"Why were you at the pub last night?" Claire asked.

"Do I need a reason?" Maria glared at her, not ready to drop her prickly edges. "Look, I know how you see me. As some old bag lady, you don't know my life."

"You were a seamstress."

"For a band," Maria said, her tone tinged with something like embarrassment. "Electric Fury. You've probably never heard of them—the lead singer's dead—but they were big in their day. I designed and made their clothes. Do you know what I got out of it?" She waited, and Claire shook her head. "Nothing. I worked for a pittance, and when I broke my wrist and couldn't work, I thought they'd help me." Her gaze dropped to the floor. "They moved on and left me behind. That killed my love for my craft because, in the end, it was all for nothing."

"I'm sorry to hear that."

"No, you're not," Maria said, picking at her nails. "All you care about is getting on with your cushy life in your lovely new house. And we're the rat pack in the way. I see you, Claire, just like I saw Jodie."

Claire faltered, unsure how to respond to the blunt assessment. It didn't feel entirely fair, but it wasn't altogether wrong either.

"I do care," Claire said quietly. "But I worked for that life. It wasn't handed to me."

"I bet you've had help?" Maria's eyes bore deeper. "I bet your comfortable parents gave you money to help get your shop up and running? And your house?" Claire squirmed, both statements true. Maria exhaled and said, "Look, all I actually wanted to say to you was that Jodie didn't have dirt on me. And I'm only saying that because I made it sound like she did. She had dirt on everyone else, but nothing concrete on me—and that drove her mad."

Claire frowned. "You were on her blackmail list."

"I didn't say she didn't try," Maria replied, her voice dropping. "She spun it like she needed a few hundred for

Lucy's art supplies. I fell for it a few times, until I realised Lucy was shoplifting canvases."

Maria exhaled sharply, her eyes darting to the walls. Claire could see the recognition as her eyes moved from one painting to another—she knew which were Lucy's.

"The only dirt Jodie had on me," Maria continued, "was my love for Lucy. She knew hurting her meant hurting me, and that fear was enough to keep me in line." Her shoulders sagged. "But it didn't mean I ever stopped watching Jodie. I never did, not for a second."

Claire's stomach tightened. "What do you mean?"

"The day Jodie died, her alarm went off early. She never got up early. I knew she was up to something, so I followed her into the garden." Maria hesitated, her voice hardening as she finished, "I overheard her talking with that wretched woman across the fence."

"Carol?" Claire confirmed.

"I didn't bother to learn her name." Maria took a deep breath, tugging at her scarf as a sheen of sweat appeared on her lined forehead. "Jodie was blackmailing her, and I think she intentionally picked your cul-de-sac. Ricky always chose our bases, and he was good at it. We could go weeks, sometimes months, without being moved along. We managed mere days at Birch Close, all because of Jodie's hubris. Her greed got the better of her. She and Carol seemed to know each other already, and Jodie *knew* Carol lived there."

"You think she picked my house to be near Carol?"

"Keep your friends close and the people you're blackmailing even closer," Maria said darkly. "Carol is as middle-class as they come, so she was the perfect target to fund Jodie's habits."

"Gambling habits, you mean?"

Maria nodded disapprovingly. "So, you know about her love for the horses. Greedy even when she had money. I've never seen someone touch so much cash and not keep hold of it long enough to use it for anything meaningful."

Claire's heart sank. That explained Carol's animosity since the squatters had arrived. No wonder she'd blamed Claire for owning the house next door—especially when a woman who'd previously terrorised her had chosen it as her next base to blackmail the neighbours.

"What was Jodie blackmailing Carol with?"

Maria glanced around, her eyes darting nervously over the crowd before she pulled Claire around the corner of an exhibition wall, away from the slow-moving tour group.

"From what I overheard—and they were whispering—it sounded like Jodie would show up every so often to remind Carol about something that happened between them a few years back. She'd make her life hell, demanding money or favours." Maria's voice dropped. "I heard Carol say she thought she'd seen the last of her, but when Jodie moved in next door, I think it broke something in Carol."

Claire's stomach churned. The thought of Carol and Jodie having a shared history—one messy enough to be worth blackmailing over—added another layer to the neighbour's already shaky alibi.

"If Carol killed Jodie, good on her," Maria said bluntly. "If anyone deserved what they got, it was Jodie."

Claire stared, taken aback. "Why are you telling me this now? You could've mentioned it before."

"Maybe I didn't trust you. Or maybe I didn't care enough to get involved." She looked back at Claire, her jaw tightening. "But now, I think you might figure this out. I know Lucy isn't a murderer—I trust her with my life. If it weren't for that girl, I would have gone my own way long ago." She sniffed as tears misted her eyes. "Believe what you want. Talk to Carol or don't. It makes no difference to me. I know I can sleep at night just fine. Now, if we're done," she said, her teary gaze searching the gallery, "I'm here to talk to the owner. Lucy deserves another go at this job. It's the happiest I've ever seen her."

Claire blinked, surprised. "After she was fired for faking paintings?"

"She never *wanted* to forge anything," Maria said, growing more irritated by the second. "Lucy has *her* style that few ever see. But Jodie saw her gift and convinced her that nobody would ever care about her art, so she might as well use it to make some money."

"A scam," Claire stated.

"Yes, that's what Jodie was good at. She pushed Lucy into it, and she didn't feel like she could say no." Maria gritted her jaw. "Not to her sister. Lucy has a gift. A *real* one, but Jodie couldn't see past the end of the week. Sometimes the end of the day. She always knew how to find someone's weakness. And then she'd bleed it dry."

"Lucy's weakness was her art?"

Maria smiled, but it left Claire feeling cold. "No. Lucy's weakness was her sister. Jodie was the only family she had left, which cancelled out anything Jodie did. And Jodie knew that." The tears returned. "You cling to anyone who feels close when you don't think you have anyone else."

Claire assessed Maria's face, understanding something about the pain in her eyes when she spoke about the young artist.

"Like you and Lucy," Claire said softly. "Who did you lose, Maria?"

Maria's lips parted, no sound coming. Claire had hit the nail on the head, and from the pained expression taking over Maria's face, she almost wished she hadn't.

"How dare you," Maria whispered, barging past.

Claire watched her go, feeling cold as warm air pumped into the gallery. Despite the answers Maria had given, she left behind a bigger question: how far would Maria go to protect Lucy?

"The owner called Lucy a sweet girl," Ryan said as they left the gallery. "Which is why I think he's holding back. He doesn't want to get her in more trouble than she's already in." He paused at the corner. "I brought up what you said about Jodie 'grassing' on Lucy. He looked puzzled."

"So, you think it was someone else?" Claire asked.

"Maybe." He leaned in, pressing a kiss to her cheek. "Just a hunch. Sorry lunch wasn't much—I thought you'd want to see what I'd pieced together about the art."

"It was certainly enlightening."

As Ryan jogged off to finish his shift at the gym, Claire swapped the cold pavement for the cosy warmth of Marley's Café.

"Claire!" Eugene called cheerily from behind the counter. "What brings you in? Tea? Coffee? A slice of Victoria sponge, perhaps?"

"I was hoping I could pop upstairs," Claire replied, glancing towards the staircase leading to the flat above. "Is Damon in?"

Eugene's smile softened. "Hasn't been out much since

yesterday. The poor lad seems to be in an awful funk. Go on up, love. You know the way."

Claire offered a grateful smile and made her way up the narrow staircase, the scent of coffee fading as she reached Damon's door. She knocked, and after a pause, the door creaked open.

Damon's face appeared, looking like he'd been wallowing in a week's worth of misery, though it had only been a day.

"Claire," he croaked, stepping aside to let her in. "Didn't expect to see you."

"Clearly," she said, sniffing. "Have you showered today?"

"I haven't done anything today."

The flat was peak Damon. A life-sized Dalek stood in one corner, its eyestalk aimed at the giant TV. But what caught Claire's attention most was the transformation of his old gaming room.

Once filled with neon lights and posters of classic movies, the room now had bunk beds pushed against the wall and shelves lined with children's books and toys. Pictures of Sally's girls were framed on the walls alongside newer photos of Damon with Sally and her kids, all smiles and laughter.

"You've turned it into a proper family flat," she said with a smile. "Look at you. The family man."

Damon shrugged, leaning against the doorframe. "It was time. Or I thought it was."

Claire turned to him, hands on her hips. "Talk to her."

"How?" He rubbed the back of his neck, avoiding her gaze. "Now she'll think I'm proposing just to get her back."

"Are you?"

"No," he said quickly. "That's not how I wanted it to happen at all. I thought I was being thoughtful, and instead, I've messed everything up."

Claire crossed her arms. "Shall I talk to her?"

Damon sighed and slumped into the recliner sofa. "That'd be the easy way out, wouldn't it? But it's not right. I need to sort this out myself. I just don't understand how Sally got to that place so quickly. How she thought I'd—"

"She's been through it, mate." Claire perched on the arm of the sofa, her gaze thoughtful. "It's what she's used to. She's had to fight to trust people, and now she's having a wobble because you started acting differently. That's all. It doesn't mean she's given up on you."

Damon looked at her with the eyes of a lovesick teenager. "You think so?"

"I *know* so," Claire said, resting a firm hand on his arm. "Can I see the ring again?"

Damon reached into his dressing gown pocket and pulled out the little leather box. He snapped it open, and Claire sighed.

"It's gorgeous," she said, admiring the diamond set in a simple band. "It's perfect."

"I modelled it after her grandmother's ring," Damon admitted, a faint blush creeping up his neck. "It was stolen years ago, but Sally had old photos."

"Oh, Damon. That's so romantic." She playfully whacked his arm with the back of her hand. "I didn't think you had it in you."

Damon let out a short laugh. "Me neither. But I shouldn't have—"

"*Talk* to her," Claire interrupted, her voice pleading. "Please, for me. I can't help but feel I helped you into this mess by not helping you out quickly enough." After a pause, she asked, "Was this the secret Christmas shopping you were doing the morning everything blew up?"

"I was trying to," he said, snapping the box shut. "I've had to go to so many shops to find something like the one in the pictures, messaging so many jewellers." He pocketed the ring. "I'll talk to her."

Claire leaned down and kissed the top of his head, and for a moment, she let her head rest there.

"Good," she said, standing up to take in the flat. "And while you're at it, shower, tidy up, and rest properly. I need you back at work on time tomorrow."

"Yes, boss," he said with a two-finger salute, a slight grin tugging at his lips. "You're becoming more like your mother every day."

"There are worse people to be," Claire said on her way to the door. "Remember, Damon—you've got this."

Claire left the café feeling like she'd finally done something right. At least Damon seemed ready to mend things with Sally. But it didn't take long for her happy bubble to be popped by a platinum blonde waving her down.

"Claire!" Gwyneth called, waving frantically from the doorway of Lilac Gifts. "Do you have a minute?"

"I do if it's about that candlestick."

Gwyneth nodded, excitement in her eyes. "I spoke to Becky, my part-time girl. She remembered a man. An older man. So, we did a little sleuthing."

"Sleuthing?" Claire raised an eyebrow, eager to hear this.

"We went on Facebook," Gwyneth said in a matter-of-fact voice. "We spent hours looking through local profiles of every man we could find. Men in their sixties, salt-and-pepper hair. And we *found* him!"

Gwyneth turned her phone towards Claire, revealing a profile picture. It wasn't any of the men on Claire's list of suspects.

"Kris Hodgkinson?" Claire muttered as his face stared back, grinning awkwardly as he held a giant fish he'd caught by a lake. "Becky is sure?"

"As sure as she can be," Gwyneth said. "He even talked

to her about the fish. She was sure he was trying to flirt with her, but he could be old enough to be her father."

"He came in on Friday and bought the candlestick?" Claire confirmed.

"Gift-wrapped."

Claire thanked Gwyneth and stepped away from the shop, her thoughts whirling. Kris Hodgkinson—she hadn't even considered him. Carol's fiery temper and defensiveness had been the obvious focus, but Kris? What possible motive could he have? The memory of their bickering in the conservatory and again at the market came to mind. Would Kris really kill to protect Carol? It didn't add up. There had to be more to this.

CHAPTER TWELVE

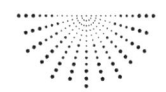

The snowman the kids had built yesterday slumped at the waist in the middle of the cul-de-sac, its crooked carrot nose drooping off its face. Starting to feel too much like that snowman the longer things went on, Claire crossed the path to Carol's house, the blackmail money from last night clutched in her hand.

She knocked, and Carol cracked the door, her face tight with distrust.

"Haven't *you* done enough damage?" Carol muttered, her simmering rage now more like light steam. "What do you want now?"

Claire held up the envelope. "I came to return this. You dropped it rushing away from The Park Inn last night. Some of it was scattered to the winds, but I think we got most of it."

Carol's eyes widened, and the hard veneer cracked. She yanked the door open, snatched the envelope, and held it close to her chest.

"You have *no* idea," Carol muttered, her voice trembling.

Claire tilted her head. "No idea about what?"

"About *this*," Carol said, gesturing vaguely. "All of this has been hell." Her words came tumbling out before she caught herself. Her expression hardened again, and she straightened, stepping back into her immaculate hallway. "It wasn't you, was it?"

"No, Carol, I wasn't blackmailing you." Claire sighed, her frustration tempered by a flicker of disbelief. How skewed must her neighbour's impression of her be? "You really don't know who it was?"

"No," Carol muttered, riffling through the money. "Thank you for returning this to me, but leave me alone."

"Carol," Claire said quickly, placing a hand on the door before it shut, "I know about the candlestick. Kris bought it for you, didn't he?"

Carol froze, the door halfway shut. "I don't know what you're talking about."

Claire stepped closer, lowering her voice. "From Lilac Gifts? It's the murder weapon that killed Jodie."

"*What?*" Carol's gaze flicked to the envelope, then

back to Claire. "I don't know anything about that," she snapped, her tone sharp but unsteady. Then she hesitated, unsure. "There was something under the tree. I thought it was a pepper grinder."

"A pepper grinder?"

Carol didn't answer. Instead, she disappeared inside. Moments later, Claire heard the muffled sounds of rummaging deep in the house.

When Carol returned, she opened the door just enough to mutter, "It's gone."

"What do you mean?"

"It's *not* there," she hissed, her eyes darting around the cul-de-sac like someone might be listening. "It was, and now it isn't. Leave me *alone*."

The door slammed, leaving Claire shivering in the cold. The candlestick Kris had bought—it had to be the murder weapon. Was Carol lying about mistaking it for a pepper grinder? Had Kris unwrapped it himself and used it on the woman blackmailing his wife? Given their heated arguments, Claire couldn't believe he'd go that far. But if Carol was being truthful, someone else must have stolen it.

The screech of tyres on ice jolted Claire from her thoughts. A car skidded to a halt on the slippery street, and Kris Hodgkinson jumped out, his focus so intent elsewhere that he barely registered her.

"Kris—"

"What?" he barked, his voice raw, almost unrecognisable.

He stormed towards the gate and kicked it open, making Claire flinch. Fumbling with his key, he marched to the front door—only to find it didn't fit. Kris, who had always prided himself on appearances and discretion, no longer seemed to care. He pounded his fists against the door, the heavy, desperate thuds reverberating around the otherwise silent cul-de-sac. These weren't the blows of a man afraid of whispers. These were the blows of a man who understood, with sickening finality, that he no longer belonged here.

Carol had changed the locks, and his car was stuffed with packed bags.

"You want me to tell the police?" Kris roared at the door. "Tell them how you made me *lie* for you?"

The alibi.

Never feeling more like her mother, Claire couldn't help but wonder which piece of straw had broken the camel's back.

LATER THAT NIGHT, AFTER FINISHING THE QUIET SHIFT AT the shop, her parents' sitting room was a mess of paper, ribbons, and stray bits of tape. Claire tried to keep up as her mother's hands flew with the speed and precision of someone who had wrapped a thousand presents before. Janet always claimed to hate wrapping, but Claire could tell she secretly loved it.

"Who thinks a candlestick is a *pepper grinder*?" Janet scoffed, snipping another piece of tape with a flourish. "She's lying."

"Mother," Claire said, warning in her tone.

"I'm *only* saying," Janet said, holding her hands up in mock surrender. "There are two explanations: either someone stole the candlestick from her house to frame her, or she's spinning you for a fool."

Claire frowned, smoothing the edges of a box.

"She's not very bright," Janet continued. "Which means she either didn't know what it was or she's playing the innocent act better than most actresses."

Ryan appeared in the doorway, leaning against the frame. "Kids are doing their homework."

"Homework? Before Christmas?" Janet shook her head in dismay. "*Barbaric.*"

"You used to say we didn't get enough when we were kids," Claire pointed out, not looking up from the ribbons she was curling.

"I remember that too," Ryan added as he came to help hold down a stubborn corner.

"I read an article about it," Janet said with a dismissive wave, as though that settled the matter.

"I've been doing some homework myself," Ryan said.

"Oh?" Claire asked.

"*Toluene*," he said. "I had a feeling I'd heard it somewhere before."

Janet's eyebrows shot up. "I didn't have you down as a nail varnish wearer, Ryan."

"Only during Amelia's salon phase," he said, wiggling his fingers and earning a laugh from Claire. He held the wrapping paper in place while she added tape. "It's also used in paint thinner, which made me think about Lucy. She's a painter, right? And we know she worked with Jodie on those forgeries. It's not impossible that she—"

"I'm not sure," Claire cut him off, feeling suddenly defensive of the girl. "Lucy wouldn't. She's vulnerable. I don't think she could kill someone, let alone her sister."

"But the truth *is* the truth," Janet interjected, not looking up from her handiwork. "That girl could be putting on an act. Playing you for a fool, like Carol might be."

"Anyone else playing me for a fool?" Claire snapped, letting go of the corner she'd been pinning down.

Janet huffed, folding her arms. "Your builders! I told you to go with the team we recommended."

"I'm not having this argument again." Claire grabbed her coat and headed for the back door. "I'm going to the bottom of the garden."

In the shed, she sat opposite her father on her plant pot, recounting her lunchtime visit to the gallery,

Gwyneth's candlestick revelation, and Carol's admission of being blackmailed—along with her insistence that she didn't know what Kris had placed under the tree.

"Hmm." Her father leaned back in his creaky chair, the faint scent of the poinsettia on his desk mingling with the chill in the air. "A lot of new pieces pointing somewhere."

"But where?"

He sighed, his eyes steady on hers. "You're not going to like this, little one."

"You think Lucy?"

"Ryan mentioned the paint thinner," he said.

"But we don't know if paint thinner killed Stuart," she said feebly. "There's just something about her—I don't think it was her."

"Or you don't want to *believe* she could." He drummed his fingers on the chair arm, his expression thoughtful. "But we do know Carol's still a suspect. Admitting her lies now doesn't change much, especially with Kris ready to confess he lied about her alibi."

"Maybe she got Kris to lie because she knew how bad it would look?"

"Perhaps," he agreed, though his frown deepened. "But I'm still stuck on what I said earlier."

"About the £10,000 Jodie wanted from Ricky?"

He nodded, groaning as he stood. "There's something in that. I can feel it." Looking for something on the desk, he said, "My gloves have gone missing. I'm sure your mother has been in here cleaning up again. Nothing is where I left it."

Back in the house, Claire kept her coat on. Instead of settling back in, she headed straight for the front door, the weight of unanswered questions spurring her on. It was time for another visit to Granny Greta's to talk to her new lodger.

"Don't be long!" Janet called from the sitting room, her voice muffled by a mouthful of tape. "There's lasagne in the oven!"

THE SHARP RAP OF CLAIRE'S KNUCKLES AGAINST HER gran's wooden door echoed in the still evening. Moments later, it creaked open, revealing Ricky. A fresh black eye bloomed across his pale face, vivid shades of purple and blue.

"She's not in," Ricky said, filling the doorway like a barricade.

"I'm here to see you," Claire replied, craning her neck to peer past him. "Gran?"

"I said she's not in," he grunted. "She's taken that dog out. What do you want?"

Claire folded her arms, her jaw tightening as she glanced through the net curtains. Her gran's usual chair in the sitting room sat empty.

"I want to know why Jodie wanted £10,000 from you," Claire said. "And don't bother denying it—I know she did."

"Jodie wanted all kinds of things she couldn't get," Ricky sneered. "Where do you think I'd find that kind of cash? I'd struggle to give her a tenner, let alone ten grand." He let out a bitter laugh, his swollen eye creasing painfully. "She was delusional."

"She must have had a reason to think you could pay."

He snorted. "Jodie just wanted me out of the way, trying to scare me into running off. But why should I? I was here first."

"Run off to keep you away from Lucy?"

Ricky's expression soured. He stepped back, ready to close the door, but Claire wedged her foot in the frame.

"Do you know where Lucy is?" she pressed, narrowing her eyes.

"Why should I?" he snapped.

"You two looked chummy at the pub the other night."

"Yeah? Things change fast around here." He rubbed at the edge of his bruised eye, muttering, "Clear off."

"How did you get that shiner?" Claire asked, unfazed.

"I fell."

"Fell?"

"Yeah, fell," His voice rose. "What's with all the questions?"

"Where's Lucy?"

"I told you," Ricky said curtly, gripping the door. "I don't know. She told me she didn't want to see me again."

"Why?"

"I don't know!" he shouted, his tone cracking with frustration. "Maybe Maria got in her head. She's no better than Jodie!"

Before Claire could press further, Ricky kicked her foot out of the doorframe and sealed it shut.

Claire stood on the pavement, her hand hovering over the handle, debating whether to try again. But she doubted she'd get anything out of him without a fight, and she wasn't in the mood. With a sigh, she turned, only to be startled by a sharp yap.

Spud, her gran's Yorkshire Terrier, bounded towards her, tiny paws kicking up a spray of snow. A moment later, Granny Greta rounded the corner, out of breath as she ran after the little dog.

"You alright, love?" Greta asked, her sharp eyes scanning Claire's face. "You look like you've been through the wars."

"I'm fine," Claire replied, leaning in to kiss her gran's cold cheek. "Have you seen that girl with the purple hair? Lucy?"

"Not since last night."

"She was here?"

Greta's lips tightened as she nodded. "She and Ricky had a proper tiff. I couldn't make out what they were saying—she's quiet even when she's angry." Her eyes narrowed. "Why?"

Claire hesitated. "Do you know how Ricky got that black eye?"

"He fell, I think. Should I know something?" Lowering her voice, she added, "He still owes me for his first week. Keeps saying it's coming, but I've got my doubts."

"I've got my doubts too," Claire admitted, glancing back at the house. "Just keep an eye on him, okay?"

"I always do," Greta said with a knowing smile. "I didn't come down with the last shower. You take care, love."

Claire nodded, watching her gran shuffle off into the snowy evening. Just last night, she'd seen Lucy and Ricky arm in arm on their way to the pub. What could have happened to turn them against each other so quickly? She couldn't picture Lucy throwing a punch. She seemed too sweet, too scared. But she was sure of one thing: Ricky's black eye wasn't from a simple fall. She needed to find Lucy, and soon.

CHAPTER THIRTEEN

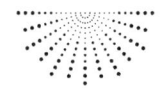

Before heading to the B&B to try and find Lucy and Maria, Claire took a detour through Starfall Park. The steep path twisted around the old observatory, its domed silhouette looming ahead—still closed for renovations after decades of neglect. Lucy's flawless imitation of Ryan's painting had captured it perfectly, but that wasn't why Claire was here.

The path levelled, leading her into 'Upper Northash'—though no such place existed on any map—where gleaming, meticulously decorated houses lined the cul-de-sac. The polished elegance made Birch Close seem like 'Lower Northash' by comparison.

Past the cul-de-sac, at the top of Park Lane, sat Northash's police station. The stone cottage curved at the corner, and if not for the row of police cars, it could easily be mistaken for just another house.

But Claire's attention was drawn back to Sally's house, halfway down the street, where festive tranquillity had crumbled into chaos. Inside, Sally's daughters, Ellie and Aria, were squabbling over a bare Christmas tree, their sharp voices spilling into the quiet evening. Sally stood between them, arms brimming with tangled tinsel, her patience wearing thin.

"*Girls!*" she barked, her tone sharp. "Why can't you get along for five minutes?"

Claire skipped knocking and let herself in. Sally spotted her and exhaled a sigh of relief, tossing the tinsel back into a box. The girls didn't glance up, too busy fighting over who got to hang the baubles.

"What's going on here?" Claire asked, crouching to their level.

Ellie and Aria immediately turned to her, ready to argue their cases. Claire raised a hand to cut them off.

"Alright, how about this?" Claire started, an idea forming. "Ellie, you take the red and gold baubles, and Aria, you do the silver and white. That way, it's coordinated and—"

"But *I* want to do the front!" Ellie cried.

"*I* want to do the front!" Aria shot back, nudging her sister aside. "You *always* do the front."

Claire thought for a moment, then rotated the tree.

"How about this? Take turns, one bauble at a time, and work together around the tree. When it's finished, you can vote on which side's the front and which is the back."

The girls hesitated, then added their baubles in silence. The absence of bickering made Sally stare at Claire like she'd just performed a Christmas miracle.

"Room for two more in your new house?" Sally asked under her breath. "When did you become the child whisperer?"

"They used to scream the house down when I babysat them."

"That's how I feel right now," Sally admitted, running a hand through her hair. "You'll have to teach me some skills."

"You're doing fine." Claire rested a hand on Sally's arm. "I've become somewhat of a negotiator between Amelia and Hugo. Kids, eh?"

With the girls peacefully occupied, Sally led Claire into the kitchen, where a tray of mince pies sat between them. They picked at the crumbling edges.

"Confession," Claire said, dusting the icing sugar from her fingers. "I saw you and Damon arguing in the street last night."

"Ugh." Sally dropped her head and gave it a few soft bangs against the gleaming marble. "Claire, I think I've messed everything up."

Rubbing her back, Claire said, "You haven't messed

everything up. I've already been to Damon. He's hopefully had a shower by now, but he's fine."

"He hasn't called."

"He's giving you space."

Sally smiled faintly. "This is where my ex-husband would send enough flowers to fill the house. Is it weird that I was expecting them?" Her smile soured. "*Dreading* them."

Still rubbing in soothing circles, Claire sensed there was more Sally wasn't telling her.

"How's it going between you two?" Claire asked gently. "You and Paul, I mean."

Sally glanced into the front room, where Ellie and Aria were finally working together on the tree. She tugged the door shut behind her and exhaled, her composure slipping.

"He's not seeing them much anymore," she said, her voice brittle. "Not since he got remarried."

"Oh, Sal."

"Two weeks ago." Sally forced a teary-eyed smile as she met Claire's gaze. "Good luck to her, I say. His fourth girlfriend since I kicked him out. She's a twenty-six-year-old 'entrepreneur', whatever that means." She took a deep breath. "But I don't care about that. Like I said—*good luck* to them both. It's just…" Her voice wavered before she said, "… he didn't tell me it was happening. Whatever, but he didn't tell the girls."

Claire sighed, the familiar resentment for Sally's ex-husband prickling in her chest. She'd never liked Paul, and he'd made no secret of disliking her, but this was a new low, even for him.

"No invite. No warning. *Nothing*. He told them when they got back and he couldn't understand why they cried their hearts out."

"That's awful."

"And guess where they tied the knot?" Sally grunted a hollow laugh. "On a beach, at the same resort where I found out he was messaging that Instagram influencer." Her voice cracked. "It's been years now, but it still feels like ripping open a scar I didn't know was still there." She sighed, picking at the foil around the mince pie. "And now Damon's started putting his phone face down, and I feel like I'm circling the same drain all over again."

Claire reached over and squeezed her hand. "Sally, I promise you—it's not like before. Damon has been acting weird, but it's not bad weird. He's up to good, I swear."

"A good thing I spoiled," Sally murmured.

"What did you spoil?"

Sally bit her lip. Then she asked, "How do you and Ryan do it? Glide through everything?"

Claire laughed softly. "We don't glide, Sally. We just… are. That's all. You and Damon have your own baggage to sort out." Lowering her voice, she added, "You know you're his first *proper* girlfriend. He's figuring things out as he goes. I know you'll work through it."

Sally straightened with a wistful sigh. "I hope you're right because, until this week, I swore I was going to marry that man someday."

Claire's smile widened. "Yeah? I think you're right."

"So, what *has* he been up to?" Sally asked, rubbing her tears away and shaking out her hair. "Please don't tell me all this drama is over a Christmas present."

"Sort of?" Claire admitted with a wry smile. "Call him and apologise. He's upset, but he's not angry *with* you. He's just confused."

"I'm confused."

"Likewise," she said, and they laughed. "But hopefully, I won't be for much longer."

After ensuring the girls were still happily decorating the tree, Claire slipped out of Sally's house, leaving her friend a little calmer.

Since she'd put the effort in to climb the hill, she stopped by the police station on the corner.

Inside, Sergeant Morgan looked up from a crossword book at the desk, her expression brightening at the sight of Claire. "Shame about those squatters. How's your dad holding up?"

"He's doing well," Claire replied, checking the empty poster-covered waiting area. "Is DI Ramsbottom around?"

"On an extended dinner break," Morgan said with a roll of her eyes. "Got something to report?"

Claire hesitated. Did she have something to report? Her thoughts drifted to Ricky's black eye. Even if his story about falling was a lie, it wasn't exactly her place to report it. Then there was Kris and Carol's fake alibi—a thread she could pull—but throwing another spanner into their mess didn't feel right, at least not yet.

"Any updates?" Claire asked instead.

"Actually, yes. A juicy one." Morgan leaned closer with a cheeky grin—she'd never been shy about sharing a tidbit with the daughter of the former DI. "Remember that bloke who keeled over at The Park Inn?"

"I was passing by," Claire replied carefully.

"Well, it turns out the poison *wasn't* in his glass," Morgan said, slapping her crossword book closed for emphasis. "Or anywhere in the pub. The poor guy must've ingested it earlier. Guilt, I reckon."

"Suicide?" Claire asked, though her mind was already racing to something else—the brown bag by the canal, with the whisky bottle sticking out. "He said it was a gift," she murmured aloud, almost to herself.

"What's that?" Morgan's brows shot up.

"I saw him earlier with a bottle of whisky," Claire said, stepping back from the counter. "The same brand I always get Dad for Christmas. Stuart said it was a gift."

Morgan's interest sharpened. "From who?"

"He didn't say." The words tumbled out quickly, her chest tightening. "Do you know what time the post office closes these days?"

Morgan glanced at her watch. "Right about now, I'd reckon."

As Claire walked down the side street next to the park, she regretted not pressing Stuart further about the gifted whisky. At the time, it hadn't seemed important. But now that he'd been poisoned, the question gnawed at her: had the whisky been laced with the chemical that killed him?

As Claire approached the darkened post office, a young lad stood at the door, fumbling with a set of keys. He barely acknowledged her, his attention fixed on The Hesketh Arms across the square, his eyes narrowing as though he couldn't wait for his post-work pint.

"Excuse me," Claire said, skipping pleasantries. "Do you stock Smith's Whisky?"

He sighed, turning to face her. "Can't you see I'm finished for the day?"

"I'm not here to buy," she assured him. "I just need to know if you still stock it."

The lad shrugged, giving her a wary look. "Yeah, as it happens."

"Were you working yesterday?"

"Why do you want to know?"

"Do you remember selling a bottle of Smith's Whisky yesterday?"

"Didn't sell one," he said flatly, jamming the keys into his pocket. "But someone did nick one."

Claire blinked. "Stole it?"

"That's what I said, isn't it?" He checked the time on his phone, eyes back on the pub. "I asked her for ID. She put on a show of patting down for it before she snatched the bottle and legged it."

"Who?" Claire's tone sharpened.

"How am I supposed to know?"

"Did you tell the police?"

"For a bottle of whisky?" He laughed. "Get real. She was just some girl."

But Claire latched onto the words. "Some girl?" she repeated, her voice low. "What did she look like?"

"Look," he said, exasperated, "I *told* you—I don't know her." He hesitated, then added, "She had purple hair."

"Purple hair," Claire echoed, already setting off. "Thanks. That really narrows it down."

The sign outside the Northash B&B declared that it was 'Home of the World's Largest Collection of Do Not

Disturb Signs.' The claim had always struck Claire as absurd and charming, much like the owner, Fergus Ferguson.

Fergus greeted her at the door with a booming laugh and a sweep of his arm. "Ah, Claire Harris! What brings you to my humble abode? Looking for a room, perhaps? I heard you had a house full. Or just admiring the signs?"

Claire couldn't help but smile. "Neither, I'm afraid. I'm looking for two guests—Maria and Lucy?"

Fergus's face lit up in recognition. "Oh, those lovely ladies! Yes, yes. They stayed for a night but checked out after breakfast this morning. They said they didn't want to overstay their welcome, especially since I wasn't charging them with it being the off-season. I don't get many bookings this time of year. Too early for the Christmas visitors and too late for the autumn walkers. Besides, they seemed like they needed a break. Very lovely, very quiet."

Claire had missed them again. Maria and Lucy had been moving through Northash like shadows, always out of reach unless she was lucky enough to bump into them.

"And they didn't say where they were going?" she asked.

"No, I didn't pry," Fergus said apologetically. "But if you find them, let them know they're welcome back here anytime! Lovely ladies."

"I hope they are," Claire murmured, smiling politely.

"While you're here, care for a tour of the museum?" Fergus asked, gesturing towards the lounge where shelves of signs gleamed under carefully placed lighting. "It's been a while since I've shown anyone around."

"Another time," Claire said quickly. "Thanks, Fergus."

Fergus sighed but nodded. "Fair enough. You're a busy woman, I know. But don't be a stranger, eh?"

"Of course," Claire said, stepping back into the cold. "Stop by the shop sometime—your next candle is on me."

As she walked away, her mind refused to budge from two details: the paint thinner and the stolen bottle of whisky. Claire didn't want to believe that Lucy could be behind the deaths, but she couldn't ignore where the facts were pointing.

Setting off to Birch Close, she had one last place to check for the artist with the purple hair.

CHAPTER FOURTEEN

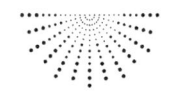

After climbing the stairs of her new house, Claire found Lucy curled up on the floor of what would soon be the master bedroom, where the faint scent of paint lingered in the air. A small canvas rested on a rag spread across the floor, surrounded by watercolours and brushes. The canvas depicted the garden view—overgrown and unremarkable, yet rendered beautifully with delicate strokes.

Lucy had fallen asleep mid-creation, her hand still loosely gripping a brush. Her soft, steady breathing was the only sound in the quiet room.

In among the equipment, Claire noticed an almost empty bottle of paint thinner. She checked the label, and there it was: *Toluene.*

Claire crouched beside her and nudged her shoulder. "Lucy?"

She stirred, blinking up at Claire with a dazed expression.

"I'm sorry," Lucy murmured, sitting up. "I just feel close to her here."

"Jodie?"

Lucy nodded, her fingers brushing the carpet. "I know she wasn't a good person. I know she did horrible things. But she was my sister. The only family I had left."

"This house reminds you of her?"

"Not really," Lucy said, shaking her head. "But the carpet—our grandfather had carpets like this. We were happy whenever we were at his house. He said it was a crime not to have something fluffy underfoot."

Claire smiled. "He'd have got on well with my mum. She's the reason this is here."

Lucy managed a small smile, her tired eyes softening, and Claire studied her carefully. If Lucy was guilty, she was either the greatest actress Claire had ever met or the most conflicted person in Northash. Claire decided to take a risk.

"I know," she said.

Lucy frowned. "Know what?"

"About the forgeries. And what you were doing in the gallery." She paused, wondering how much she should reveal. "And I know you stole a bottle of whisky from the post office."

Lucy skirted back to the window. "So what?"

"I saw Stuart with that same bottle of whisky before he died," she continued, "and he was poisoned with a chemical found in paint thinner. I couldn't help but notice you're running a little *thin*." Sighing, she added, "I think it's time to tell the truth."

Lucy froze, her expression clouding over. Before she could respond, creaking on the landing made Claire turn around. Maria filled the doorway.

Claire's heart shuddered as the door clicked shut behind Maria. The sound reverberated in the small room, far louder than it should have been. Maria leaned back against the door, her posture casual, but her eyes were anything but. They were sharp, focused, and locked on Claire, but Claire's wandered somewhere else—to Maria's hands, specifically her bloody knuckles.

"I fell over," Maria said, tensing her fingers. "Happens more than you'd think at my age."

"Funny, Ricky said the same thing," Claire countered as Maria stuffed her hands into her pockets. "Did you punch him?"

"I told you all I was going to tell you in the gallery earlier," Maria grunted. "Why are you here?"

"Aside from this being my home?"

Maria shifted, kicking away from the door. "We'll be

gone by morning. Just one more night. We're leaving Northash."

"Running from Northash, you mean?" Claire stood her ground on the fluffy carpet. "I know Lucy stole a bottle of whisky that I think led to Stuart's death."

Maria's eyes darted from Claire to Lucy, but Claire couldn't read her conflicted expression.

"You know *nothing*," Maria muttered, her voice taking on a dark edge that Claire hadn't heard before. "Lucy stole that bottle for me." She flung open the door. "Time for you to stop sticking your nose where it isn't wanted, Claire." Averting her eyes, she added, "Like I said, we'll be gone by morning."

Claire stepped towards the door, stopping when she came face-to-face with Maria. Their eyes met, and Claire searched them—tired, hollow, and restless. At the gallery, Claire had been sure Maria was being truthful. Now, she wasn't so confident.

"You'd never have asked Lucy to steal for you," Claire said, looking back at Lucy as she packed her painting supplies. "You care too much, Maria."

"You don't know us," Maria replied, her tone guarded.

"No," Claire admitted with a sigh. "I don't."

Downstairs, the house was quiet, its stillness unsettling. Claire stood in the kitchen, unable to look away from the floorboards. It was hard to believe that just days ago, Jodie's body had lain there, the scene now scrubbed clean of all evidence.

Her mind wandered back to the night they'd arrived, the kids laughing and throwing snowballs, their voices rising in playful arguments over who got which bedroom. She'd held Ryan's hand, their hearts brimming with excitement and hope. It had felt like the start of something new—a promise of fresh beginnings.

But then Ricky had stumbled through the front door, and nothing had been the same since.

She blinked, pulling herself back to the present. The floorboards gleamed, sanded and unblemished as though Jodie had never been there.

She shifted her foot, the floor creaking beneath her weight.

And then a crunch. She froze. The sound was faint but distinct, unnatural against the smooth wood. Slowly, she lifted her foot, revealing a small, misshapen object jammed in the gap between the boards. She bent down, squinting as her fingers brushed against its jagged edges. She plucked it free and held it up to the light.

A pinecone.

It was dried and brittle, rough to the touch. Her mind

raced. There had been no pinecones in the house that morning. The crime scene cleaners had swept through, scrubbing every trace of Jodie's presence from the room.

And yet here it was, lying in the exact spot where Jodie's blood had pooled.

Her stomach twisted. This wasn't a coincidence.

Next door, Claire charged straight for Carol's bin, where the fallen wreath had been. It had been collected, leaving an empty bin at the kerb with only the tang of the last fortnight's rubbish. Claire crossed the path to Carol's front door, bracing for another confrontation with her difficult neighbour.

When Carol opened the door, her face was pale, her eyes red-rimmed. She looked smaller, shrinking like the past days had caught up with her.

"*Again*? Come to gloat?" Carol said, closing the door to only an inch. "Whatever it is, I'm not in the mood."

"I've come about this," Claire said, holding up the pinecone. "It was lodged between the floorboards, and I couldn't think of where it could have come from, but then I remembered your wreath."

Carol shrunk back. "I don't have a wreath, as you can see."

"Not anymore, but you did," Claire said, cramming her shoe in the gap before Carol shut her out. "It fell off when you slammed the door the night you screamed at me about the squatters."

"I'm *sorry*, alright? Is that what you want to hear?"

"Sorry you shouted at me for no reason, or sorry you killed Jodie?"

Carol's eyes narrowed through the gap. "I didn't. I couldn't—"

"Then how did *this* come to be in my house?" Claire urged, forcing the door open further. "*This* is what you were digging for in my leaves the other morning. I think this must have been on your doorstep and got lodged in your shoe, and then you walked it over there before you—"

"I *didn't*," she insisted.

"You lied about your alibi, and two people saw you arguing with Jodie over the fence about—"

Carol gasped, her face twisting in panic. Before Claire could react, Carol grabbed her arm and yanked her inside, shutting the door behind them.

The force shoved Claire against the wall, her breath hitching as Carol's hands pressed her shoulders firmly in place.

"Who told you about the affair?" Carol demanded, her voice a frantic whisper. "*Who?*"

"No one," Claire managed, her heart racing. She hadn't known about any affair, and it would have been the last thing she'd have guessed. "But Maria might know."

Carol froze. "Who? Is she in the choir? The WI?"

"No," Claire said, her voice steadying. "She's next door. One of the squatters. Are you going to kill her after you kill me?"

Carol's expression twisted with disgust and confusion, her face contorting as if she were trying to process the unthinkable. She stepped back, her trembling hands reaching for the chair by the telephone. She sank into it, her head falling into her hands as the first sob escaped her.

Claire felt uncomfortable, glancing at the door. She could leave—*should* leave—but Carol's heaving shoulders kept her rooted to the spot. She was still her neighbour.

Claire plucked a tissue from a nearby box and held it out. "Do you want to talk about it?"

"No!" Carol snapped, though she snatched the tissue and blew her nose. Her voice wavered as she added, "It was *one* night. A mistake. A stupid mistake." Her eyes searched Claire's. "Have you told your mother?"

"No."

"Please, don't." Carol's voice cracked. "I don't want to give her more ammunition. If this gets out—"

"That's why you were paying Jodie," Claire confirmed. "To keep her quiet?"

"I paid Jodie… and paid her… and *paid* her," Carol said, her voice rising with each repetition. "She wouldn't stop popping up. She said it was the last time *every* time, and then—like a cockroach—she came back. And then she was next door. It was like waking up in a nightmare."

"What happened between you?" Claire asked.

Carol buried her face in her hands again. "It was *one* night. I found out Kris and his boss were back to their after-work activities. So, I went to The Park Inn to drown my sorrows away from prying eyes, and I met this younger woman who knew just what to say. She told me I didn't need a man upsetting me. She was so charming, so understanding." Her voice broke as she continued, "Before I knew it, I was acting so unlike myself. And I swore I was going to leave Kris."

Carol laughed bitterly, the sound hollow. "But the next morning, Kris cooked breakfast and bought me flowers. I knew it was guilt, but I just wanted to believe we could make it work. I thought I'd got even with him, that we could start fresh. And then the blackmail letters started turning up."

"You paid to keep your marriage alive," Claire said.

Carol nodded, her laughter sharper now. "It would have taken an atomic bomb to reignite our spark. Do your parents sleep in separate rooms?"

"No," Claire replied.

"I didn't think so," Carol muttered, dabbing her eyes. "Kris said they probably did when he suggested we give it a go. He couldn't stand to be around me anymore. I should have ended things sooner, but I couldn't admit defeat. I don't even know why I'm telling you all this. I've never told anyone."

Claire handed her another tissue, resting a gentle hand on her knee. "I have a friend who was in a similar situation. She kept giving it another go until she couldn't, and it left her in a bad place. I won't pretend it's all plain sailing, but she's better now. Most of the time."

Carol nodded, her breathing slowing.

"But," Claire said, holding up the pinecone, "how did this end up in my house if you didn't kill Jodie?"

Carol didn't answer right away. She rose from her chair, her movements slow and deliberate, and walked through the kitchen into the conservatory. Claire followed, and from where Carol stood beside the unlit Christmas tree, she could see straight into Claire's kitchen.

Carol's voice broke the silence, flat and measured. "When we were talking over the fence, I told her I was *done*—done playing her games. Done with her demands. I wasn't going to pay her another penny. I told her if she told anyone, I was going to kill her."

Claire's stomach twisted. "Did you mean it?"

"Perhaps. Maybe I thought I would. I was *desperate*, Claire. I went next door with a knife in my pocket, and I wanted her to believe me. Wanted her to feel as scared as she was making me." She looked down at her hands, clenching around the handle of an invisible knife. "But someone beat me to it."

"You found Jodie dead on the floor?" Claire pressed, unable to believe her ears. "Why didn't you raise the alarm?"

"I was relieved at first." Carol stared as though she could see herself looking at Jodie's body in the kitchen next door. "But I was at the scene of a murder. I *couldn't* be. How would it look? They'd kick me out of the choir, and one look at the withdrawals from my savings account, all fingers would point my way. I knew I might stand a chance if I kept my head down and ignored her." She glared at Claire over her shoulder. "But you're *just* like your mother. So nosey, always trying to get in my business." She exhaled, clenching her eyes. "I asked Kris if he bought me that candlestick. He said he did because he 'didn't know what to buy me'." She laughed. "I don't even like candles. He *knows* that."

"Did he—"

"Kill Jodie for me?" Another laugh, colder this time. "No. He didn't leave the house. I checked our cameras when he came back earlier to get the rest of his stuff. He didn't leave, but someone came in."

"Who?" Claire gulped.

"I don't know," she said in a small voice. "They were

dressed in black, but they searched the conservatory. I don't think they knew what they were looking for. They dug under the tree, found the wrapped candlestick, weighed it in their hands, and left."

Claire wasn't sure if she should believe Carol, but she found that she did. Claire leaned forward, her heart aching for the woman who had always been her parents' frosty neighbour, never actually knowing anything about her beyond what she revealed on the doorstep.

"I'm sorry," Claire said, wrapping her arms around Carol. For a moment, she resisted, stiff and guarded, but then she melted into the embrace, her sobs muffled against Claire's shoulder.

"Do you think you could've actually stabbed Jodie?" Claire asked, pulling back.

Carol shook her head, wiping at her eyes. "I can't even kill a spider. But I wanted her to *think* I would. To feel what I felt."

"You were desperate," Claire stated. "But there was someone else who was more desperate. Have you given the police the video footage?"

"And admit that I forgot to lock the back door?" Carol sighed. "I suppose I'll have to, won't I?"

"Don't worry." Claire winked, passing Carol another tissue. "It happens to the best of us."

"I just want things to go back to normal," Carol said. "Not that I know what normal is now."

"Go forward, Carol," Claire said. "And normal is so overrated."

Carol nodded, her tears subsiding as she looked up at Claire. "You're going to figure out who it was, aren't you?"

"I'm going to try," Claire promised.

CHAPTER FIFTEEN

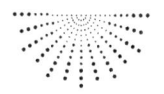

*I*n the shed at the bottom of the garden, Claire perched on her usual terracotta plant pot. The coffee cupped in her palms was almost cold. Across from her, her father sat at his desk, repotting the poinsettia he'd picked up at the supermarket.

"They never put the right mix in," Alan said, shaking his head as he scooped fresh soil from a bag. "A little love, and I'll have this lasting through February."

Claire tried to smile, but it felt like too much effort. Her mind was a mess of conflicting stories and scattered clues. She'd told her father about the pinecone, about Carol's blackmail and the missing candlestick, but none of it felt like it fit together.

"I don't think Carol's guilty," she said eventually, her

voice low. "But I do think the murderer stole that candlestick from under her tree."

Alan patted the soil down, his focus on the plant. "Why not use something more to hand?"

Claire frowned, considering. "Maybe they wanted to throw suspicion onto everyone connected to Jodie? The guitar string, the paint, the hammer, Maria's thread…"

Alan paused, glancing up at her. "What thread?"

"Ramsbottom never mentioned it?"

"No. He was here earlier trying to pick my brains, but I've no idea what's going on."

"Maybe he left it out because it's such a small piece of evidence," Claire suggested, drawing her knees closer. "Or he didn't notice it. It's not like he found the murder weapon or the pinecone."

"If he had, he might have had enough to arrest Carol and charge her." He dusted soil from his fingers, his expression thoughtful. "Are you sure she's innocent, little one? She might be pulling the wool over your eyes."

"Maybe," Claire admitted, sipping the cold coffee. "But when Carol thought the candlestick was a pepper grinder, her confusion seemed real. And tonight, she broke down. She admitted she wanted to kill Jodie, but she didn't."

They sat in silence for a moment, the only sound the soft scraping of soil as Alan finished rehousing the poinsettia into a shiny red pot. Claire's gaze drifted across the workbench, landing on the bottle of whisky near the edge.

"That's the same brand Stuart had," she said, remembering what happened before she'd found the pinecone. "Lucy stole it from the post office, but Maria claimed it was for her."

Alan set the pot aside. "So, if it wasn't Carol, it must have been one of those two?"

Claire hesitated. "Did Ramsbottom say anything else?"

"There were boot prints leading to and from Jodie's body," he revealed, leaning back in his creaky chair. "Work boots, size eleven. Ramsbottom thinks they were Stuart's." He straightened, giving her a meaningful look. "But if Stuart killed Jodie, who killed Stuart?"

"Sergeant Morgan thinks Stuart took his own life."

Alan shook his head, not convinced. "Weird way to do it. People don't often drink a toxic amount of paint thinner and then go sit in the pub until they keel over."

Claire drank the last of the cold coffee, her mind spinning with questions she couldn't answer. The shed felt too small, too cluttered.

There was a sharp knock at the shed door.

Alan glanced up from tidying his workbench. "That'll be Ramsbottom back for round two."

But it wasn't Ramsbottom.

Maria stood in the doorway, looking uncertain but resolute.

"Janet said I could come down here," she said, still on the other side of the threshold. "I hope I'm not interrupting."

"Come in," Claire offered, stepping aside.

"Get yourself warm," Alan added, wheeling back to make more space. "There's a bite in the air tonight."

"It's not that cold," Maria replied, stepping into the shed. She took in the cluttered space as she unzipped her coat. "I wanted to apologise, Claire. For how I spoke to you earlier. I'm just tired of the questions, the poking around."

Claire tilted her head. "And surprised to hear Lucy stole that bottle of whisky?"

"You noticed." Maria nodded, her brows heavy over those tired eyes. "She doesn't drink. Never has. Stuart did, though, but Lucy swears she didn't give him the bottle."

"You're saying someone else did?" Alan asked curiously.

Maria glanced down, pulling her hand from her pocket to inspect her knuckles. She winced at the sight of them—red, raw, and swollen.

"Oh, dear," Alan said, already pulling a first aid kit from one of his many drawers. "Let me patch those up."

"It's fine," Maria protested.

"No, no. Sit." He gestured to Claire's plant pot in the corner.

Maria hesitated before reluctantly perching on the edge. Alan handed her a fig roll, and when she accepted it, he set to work cleaning her grazed knuckles. She ate quickly, so he handed her another.

"It's been a while since anyone's done anything like this for me," Maria admitted quietly, watching Alan work. "I'm usually the one taking care of others."

"You look after Lucy," Claire said.

"I have to," Maria replied, her head dipping. "She's too trusting."

"You punched Ricky," Claire said, sighing, "didn't you?"

Maria froze, her eyes darting warily to Alan.

"*Retired* detective." He offered a reassuring smile. "Anything said in this shed stays here—like a confession booth."

"As sacred as one," Claire added with a smile. "I've confessed my sins in here a few too many times."

Maria nodded heavily, unable to look at either of them. "I punched him," she admitted. "I went to the gallery to try and get Lucy her job back. Without Jodie, she wouldn't have anyone standing in her way. I tried to explain what Jodie had done, but the owner didn't know what I was talking about. He knew about the forgeries, but Jodie didn't tell him about them." She exhaled, wincing as Alan applied a fresh plaster across her knuckles after cleaning the area. "It was Ricky."

"*What?*" Claire's voice rose. "Ricky told me it was Jodie."

"He told Lucy that too," Maria said, her lips curling into a snarl. "But the gallery owner described Ricky as clear as day. The hair, the smirk—he even had his guitar with him. I confronted Ricky, and he admitted it—said *I* was getting in his way. That I was poisoning Lucy's mind, that I was just like Jodie. It all felt so manipulative. I've known men like him before, and there's no way to get through to them, so I decked him." Her lips lifted into something of a smile. "And I don't regret it."

"Ricky said Lucy called things off with him," Claire pointed out.

"She did," Maria confirmed. "Last night. He grabbed her wrist, demanding to know where her paintings were stashed. Lucy told him it was over and ran. She didn't think he'd look at your house, so we decided to spend one more night there while we figured out our next moves." She turned to Claire and said, "We are running, but not from the police—from *him*."

"Why did he want Lucy's paintings?" Alan asked.

"So *he* could sell them," Maria muttered, exhaling as though she couldn't believe it. "Ricky wanted to use her for her talents, just like Jodie did." She paused, noticing the boots by the door. "Where'd you get those?"

"They're not mine," Alan said, shuffling to pick them

up. "Far too big. I did wonder when my dear wife tripped over them the other day."

"They're Stuart's," Maria said.

"Stuart said they went missing," Claire said, remembering when the police had dragged Stuart downstairs. "The morning Jodie was killed, he claimed someone had moved them."

Alan's face hardened. "What are they doing here?"

Another moment from the night before Jodie's murder flashed through Claire's mind. She'd been out in the snow after dark, snooping around the house to see what the squatters were up to. Jodie had thrown Ricky out again, and Claire hadn't wanted to see him cast out in the cold.

"Dad, did you find your gloves?" Claire asked, suddenly paying attention to every inch of the cramped shed. "You said you thought Mum had been in here cleaning, but we both know she avoids this place like the plague."

"I found them," he said, tugging open a drawer to show her. "But they weren't where I put them. Quite a few things have moved around, as it happens, but I didn't want to say anything on account of my age."

"It's not your age," Claire said, trying to catch her breath as her heart sped up. "I told Ricky about this shed and offered it to him the night before Jodie died. He ran off, but what if he came back? To stay close?"

"Ricky told Lucy to steal that bottle of whisky," Maria said in a small voice, croaking in her throat. "It took Lucy a while to tell me, but she admitted he put her up to it yesterday morning."

"*He* told me about your thread being at the scene," Claire thought aloud, her eyes narrowing as the pieces fell into place. "Ramsbottom never mentioned anything about any thread. Guitar string, paint, the blackmail note, the hammer… but no thread."

"I was never questioned about any thread," Maria said, shaking her head as she hoisted herself off the plant pot with a groan. "This is the first I've heard about it."

Claire shot to her feet, urgency driving her across the shed.

"Where are you off to, little one?" Alan called.

"To Gran's," she said, opening the door to the cold wind. "Call Ramsbottom. Tell him *everything*."

She burst through the back door into the kitchen as her mother polished the marble island with a cloth.

"Claire! *Shoes*!" Janet cried, trying to whip Claire with the rag. "I've *just* mopped!"

"I'll sort it later, Mother!" she replied, almost slipping before she bombed down the hallway. "Sorry!"

Ryan paused on the stairs, already in his pyjamas for the evening.

"Ah, *there* you are," he said with a tired smile. "The kids are finally down. Hugo took some convincing, but

Amelia helped for once." He leaned against the banister. "Can you feel the peace? How about we have a normal night? Just us, a film, and the sofa?"

Claire slowed, the warmth of his offer almost pulling her in. She stepped on tiptoes, kissing him through the railing.

"Great idea." But she ran for the front door, grabbing her coat from the hook. "I won't be long. Line something good up."

"Where are you going?"

"To have a word with Granny Greta," Claire called over her shoulder, flashing him a worried smile. "She needs to be more careful about who she takes pity on in the chippy…"

CHAPTER SIXTEEN

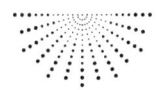

*C*laire struggled to catch her breath as she reached her gran's cottage. She rattled the door handle—it was locked. She banged her knuckles against the wood. No answer. The cottage stood silent, its windows dim.

She tried to slow her breathing, her heart hammering out of control. Peering through the net curtains at the front window, she spotted her gran slumped in her armchair by the three-bar fire, its dull red glow casting a faint warmth over her face.

For a moment, Claire froze—Granny Greta looked so still. Too still.

Spud, the terrier, jumped up from the rug, barking and wagging his tail. Claire knocked on the glass again, harder this time. Her gran stirred, her head lolling to one side.

"*Gran!*" Claire called, but there was no discernible response.

The dog barked louder as panic surged in Claire's chest. She tried the door again, rattling the handle and pushing her shoulder against it. She wasn't strong enough to make it budge.

"Little one?" Her father's voice called out. Claire turned to see him hurrying towards her, having just parked across the street near the gallery. "Is she alright?"

"I—I don't know," Claire stammered.

Swallowing her fear, she darted to the end of the street, rounding the corner to the back garden. She climbed over old furniture, ignoring the scrape of a nail against her coat. The back door loomed ahead—locked, like the front. But Claire knew her gran well—knew the gnome with the ridiculous moustache wasn't just decoration.

She crouched, flipping the ceramic figure onto its side. The key glinted with the worms in the mud beneath.

Claire let herself in, shutting the door behind her. The cottage was warm and silent except for the faint hum of the electric fire. Spud's barking echoed louder as she hurried into the sitting room.

"Gran?" Claire dropped to her knees by the armchair. Her gran's eyelids fluttered, her face pale and slack.

"Gran, wake up. Have you taken something?" Claire's hands shook as she fumbled her phone from her pocket and dialled for an ambulance. The operator assured her the paramedics would be there soon, but no amount of time would be quick enough for Claire "Granny... *please...*"

She groaned, her head tipping back against the chair. Claire gripped her hand, her eyes darting around the room. Above her, a floorboard creaked.

The sound cut through the silence, sharp and deliberate. Her heart thudded, torn between checking upstairs and staying at her gran's side.

The creaking grew louder, heavier, like footsteps pacing.

"Little one?" her father called through the front door. "Is she alive?"

Claire scrambled to unlock the door, sliding back the chain. She flung the door open before her father hobbled inside, panting—he'd been in such a rush he hadn't brought his cane.

"I think he's up there," Claire said, her foot already on the bottom step, her gaze lingering on her gran. "I've called an ambulance—stay with her. I need to check upstairs."

"Claire, don't—"

But she was already climbing.

The worn carpet muffled her hurried steps as her

fingers brushed the rough wallpaper, family photos passing by in her peripheral vision. The air felt colder here, heavier. At the top of the stairs, her gran's bedroom door stood ajar.

She pushed it open.

Ricky stood in the middle of the room, stuffing jewellery and trinkets into a duffel bag. The drawer of the nightstand lay overturned, clothes and papers scattered across the floor.

"Ah, Claire," Ricky said brightly, his sly grin broadening. "We have to stop meeting like this."

Her stomach churned. "What did you give her?"

"She's fine," he said, his tone breezy as he shut the bag. "Just something in her tea to help her sleep, that's all. She'll wake up tomorrow after the best sleep of her life. No need to get worked up." He slung the bag over his shoulder, but Claire filled the doorway. "Don't make this harder than it needs to be."

"You drugged my gran."

"I did what I had to do," he said, eyes narrowing on her. "To survive."

"Who told you about Maria's thread being left at the crime scene?" she asked, and he offered no reply. "Was it the police? Or did you know because *you* put it there?"

Ricky dropped his head, heaving out a sigh.

"Who died and put you in charge?" he asked, glancing

up at her through his brows, the last trace of humour leaving his eyes. "Get out of my way."

"Jodie died," Claire said, unwilling to move. "Everything comes back to her. You hated her. You couldn't stand how she treated Lucy, how she undermined you. You tried to be their leader before she showed up. You wanted her gone, didn't you?"

Ricky's face twisted at the accusation. "You don't know what you're talking about."

"Don't I?" Claire took another step forward, her voice rising. "I know you've been playing everyone. You've tried to frame everyone. You put Maria's thread there. Stuart's hammer, Carol's candlestick, even your guitar string. You used Stuart's boots, and I think you took up my offer to sleep in my dad's shed." She paused, swallowing a lump that wouldn't budge. "You even tried to pin it on Lucy with her paints on Jodie's clothes. Just in case?"

"I *love* her." Ricky's composure cracked. He dropped the bag onto the bed and ran a hand through his hair, his breath coming in shallow gasps. "You… you don't understand."

"Then make me understand," Claire demanded. "Because here's what I see: you killed Jodie to get rid of the one person keeping you apart from her sister. You killed Stuart when he figured it out. I overheard him talking to someone on the phone. Someone who was trying to blackmail him." She dropped her head, laughing as she put the pieces together. "You tried to blackmail him, but he had your card marked."

"He was *guessing*," he snapped. "He didn't know anything."

"But you still killed him," Claire continued, moving closer. "You convinced Lucy to get you a bottle of whisky, and you filled it with *her* paint thinner before you gifted it to Stuart, once again trying to frame her."

"We were going to be far away," he muttered, his eyes darting from the door to the window. "It wouldn't have mattered, but she wouldn't—"

"Wouldn't let you sell her paintings for your getaway?" Claire jumped in, ducking to meet his eyes. "That's not love, that's manipulation. Was blackmailing Carol a backup plan?"

"It's not like she didn't have it to give!" he cried, tossing his hands out. "Jodie got *thousands* out of her." His shoulders slumped, the fight draining out of him. "We would have been *happy*. Do you think I *wanted* any of this? I didn't plan it, alright? I didn't sit down and think, 'Oh, today's the day I kill Jodie.' It just *happened*. She was always trying to get rid of me. I had a good thing with Lucy before she ruined everything."

"Explain," she said coldly.

"She was *suffocating* us," Ricky said, pacing through the mess he'd caused. "She treated Lucy like she was worthless. She's so talented, Claire, and she was *ruining* her. I wanted her gone. I wanted Lucy to see how much better life could be without Jodie." He met her eyes, searching for understanding. "Where was I supposed to find £10,000? When Jodie found out…"

Claire sighed, another piece of the puzzle clicking into place. "Jodie knew you told the gallery about Lucy."

"She had to figure out why her cash cow lost her route to market," Ricky spat, smashing his fists down on the dresser. The remaining framed pictures toppled over. "I just wanted to free Lucy. You didn't see her. Jodie had her working day and night, painting like she wasn't even human, always promising the money would save them and that all of Lucy's sacrifices would be worth it one day." He shook his head, a crazed look in his eyes. "But that day was never going to come unless *someone* did *something*. I tried to convince Lucy that we could make it without her, but she was so attached to that *sponge*."

"Her sister," Claire clarified.

"Like Jodie cared!" he cried. "Lucy made Jodie a small fortune, and she threw it away."

"Jodie couldn't pick the winning horse," Claire said, stepping backwards as she heard footsteps entering the cottage below. "And now she's dead."

"I had no choice," Ricky said, his voice cracking. "She was never going to give Lucy the life she'd promised. It was all a lie to keep Lucy flogging her fakes, all so Jodie could keep wallowing, and gambling, and extorting, and *controlling*. Not just Lucy, but all of us. It was all just some sick game to her. She acted like we were her playthings… her *prisoners*." He let out a roar, doubling over. "She had nothing else, so she had to make our lives as miserable as hers. She kept us down every time she had a chance to lift us, and I told Jodie as much the night she kicked me out. I told her we were sick of it, but the others wouldn't back me. Why would they? Jodie had put food in their bellies and found them a house with nice carpets. They were all so short-sighted. I could see the future without her, and I knew she wouldn't be missed."

Ricky sat on the edge of the bed, his hands limp in his lap. For a moment, he seemed smaller, the confidence drained from his sharp grin. Claire stood by the doorway, keeping her distance.

"I did what I had to," he said, staring into his open palms as if measuring the candlestick's weight. "I let myself into Carol's conservatory and found something heavy. I thought Jodie would be in bed—she never woke up early. But then I saw her talking to Carol over the fence, squeezing in an early blackmail session."

He paused, his lip curling. "I waited in the kitchen for her to come back. When she did, she had that look on her face—that smug smile she always wore. But then she saw me. Saw what I was holding. That wiped the smile right off." His voice cracked, and his hands trembled. "I'd never seen her look scared before. She tried to run, so I hit her. She went down in one. And before I knew it, I was running around, gathering things to leave near her body." He exhaled shakily, his eyes hollow as he met Claire's gaze. "Jodie was strangling Lucy—creatively, financially, emotionally. If I hadn't stepped in, she would've ruined her completely."

He leaned forward, his voice heavy. "So yeah, I lied. I manipulated. And I've got blood on my hands. But everything I did, I did to save her."

"You didn't have to drag everyone else into your mess."

"I never dragged *you* in." He met her gaze, his face weary. "You did that on your own. I didn't want this to spiral out of control. But once Jodie was gone, the ground fell from under me. Everything I did was to protect Lucy, to give her a chance to be free. And… I've ruined everything."

The faint wail of sirens in the distance pulled Claire back to the doorway. She gripped the frame as Ricky stared at the floor, defeated. His eyes darted to the window.

"It's over," Claire said, regaining her strength. "You can try to run, and I won't chase you." She sighed, extending a hand towards him. "But come downstairs, hand yourself in, and don't let Lucy spend her days sleeping with one eye open, waiting for you to show up. If you truly love her, give her that peace."

Ricky didn't take long to decide. He reached out and grabbed Claire's hand. For a moment, they stood at arm's length, gripping tightly. Claire wondered what might have become of the boy thrown out of his band if he'd taken a different path—if he'd never met Lucy or Jodie. Would he have been driven to kill, or had his infatuation with saving Lucy driven him to his desperate acts?

When the police officers rushed in, Ricky didn't resist. He allowed himself to be handcuffed face down against the bed and led downstairs. His fight was over. Claire followed them down.

In the sitting room, Greta began to stir, her eyelids fluttering open.

"I feel drunk as a skunk," Greta mumbled, blinking up at Claire. "What's all the noise?"

Claire smiled, brushing a strand of hair from her gran's eyes.

"Just a little eviction," she said, exhaling deeply. "You need to vet your next lodger a bit better."

As Ricky was taken away, Claire felt both relief and sorrow. The storm had passed, but the scars it left behind would take longer to heal. Ricky might have been right— few people would miss Jodie—but she was still Lucy's sister. That scar would never fully fade.

But for now, Lucy was free. They all were.

SPICED ORANGE SUSPICION

The street outside Granny Greta's house buzzed with quiet chaos. The news had spread quickly, as it always did in Northash. A small crowd had begun to gather in the road, murmuring to each other in hushed tones. Claire stood with DI Ramsbottom, the days of worry lifting from her chest.

Ramsbottom held his notepad, flipping through the pages. "Well, Claire," he said, his voice carrying a note of respect, "Credit where credit is due. After I heard about the paint thinner, I was putting together a case to have Lucy arrested. Good work."

"It all worked out in the end," she said.

"That it did," he admitted with a slight chuckle. Then his tone sobered. "We've got him *with* a confession, and him trying to rob your gran on the way out was the cherry on top. There'll be no wiggle room for his defence."

Claire wasn't going to worry about what happened next. It had been over for her when she'd watched the police drive away with Ricky handcuffed in the backseat.

At the end of the street, Lucy and Maria appeared, making their way through the onlookers. Lucy's wide, searching eyes met Claire's, and her face crumpled.

"It's true, isn't it?" Lucy asked, her voice barely above a

whisper. "It was him. *Ricky*. He killed my sister. He killed Stuart."

Claire nodded. "He confessed everything. Did you know?"

"No," Lucy replied quickly. "But after that bottle of whisky, I just didn't trust him anymore."

She curled over in a fit of tears, and Maria caught her, pulling her into a protective hug. Her sobs were raw, unrestrained, the tears streaking her cheeks as she clung to Maria. She seemed to have been holding them in since the moment she'd seen Jodie's body on the kitchen floor.

"I thought Ricky was different," Lucy choked out. "I thought he was *better*."

"Yeah," Maria said softly, stroking her hair. "They all make you think that, don't they?"

Claire swallowed hard, looking away to give them a moment.

The sound of hurried footsteps drew Claire's attention, and she turned to see Ryan sprinting down the lane, still in his pyjamas. Relief flooded her as he reached her, out of breath.

"You told me to line up a film!" he cried, pulling her into a tight hug. "And then I hear there's been an arrest. Claire, are you okay?"

She nodded against his chest. "I'm okay. I promise. Relieved, actually. It's done. We can go home."

Ryan leaned back, his hands on her shoulders as he searched her face. "Are you sure? You don't look okay."

"I'm sure," she said, managing a smile. Then she turned him towards the gallery across the road. "Speaking of moving on, what are you going to do about the gallery? Are you going to take the job?"

Ryan hesitated, caught off guard by the question. "It's still bad timing."

Before Claire could respond, Lucy, still clutching Maria's hand, wiped her face and interjected, her voice shaky but sincere. "The commission on sales is excellent," she said. "I should know."

A small, awkward laugh rippled through the group, breaking the tension left behind from uncovering the truth. Claire squeezed Ryan's arm.

"You don't have to decide right now," she said, "but you'll have to decide soon."

The sound of carol singers warming up by the clock tower drifted over, their voices a soothing balm after the chaos. Eugene's bellowing stuck out in the crowd. A soft harmony of *Silent Night* filled the cold night air, and Claire slipped her hand into Ryan's, leaning her head on his shoulder. The crowd began to disperse, the drama of the night fading into the background as Northash returned to its quiet rhythm.

A few hours later, Ricky might have fled with Granny Greta's precious things, never to be seen again. She might not have been able to save Jodie or Stuart, but her timing had stopped him in his tracks.

"Before Christmas, you said," Ryan said, pressing a kiss to her forehead. "You did it."

Claire smiled, her heart swelling with the weight of everything that had happened—and the relief of knowing it was over.

They stood together, hand in hand, as the carol singers' voices carried over the square, a strange saga finally drawing to a close.

BACK AT BIRCH CLOSE, CLAIRE PUSHED OPEN THE DOOR TO the guest room, where Amelia and Hugo were tucked up in their single beds. The faint glow of Hugo's Switch lit up his face while Amelia was bundled under a patchwork quilt.

Claire knelt beside Hugo, her voice soft. "Guess what?" she whispered. "It's all sorted."

"Really?" Hugo paused his game, his eyes widening. "Does that mean we can move in?"

"I think so." Claire nodded, brushing a stray curl from his forehead. "The sooner the better."

"Tomorrow?" Hugo grinned, excitement bubbling in his voice. "Can I have the bigger bedroom?"

Claire winked. "Maybe. Don't tell Amelia."

"I *heard* that," Amelia grumbled, not asleep after all. "We'll flip a coin for it."

Ryan appeared behind Claire, his arms wrapping around her waist as he leaned down to kiss her head. "That sounds like a plan to me."

"I still don't know why you *want* to live in that empty box!" Janet chimed in from the hallway, balancing a precarious stack of papers on her way back from the computer room. "You could stay here until next year."

"We could," Claire said, joining her mother on the landing. "And it's always here for us." She glanced back at Ryan, who was watching her with quiet amusement. "But it's *our* bare shell."

"Well, you'll want to get in before more squatters move in," she quipped, thrusting the stack of papers into Claire's hands. "Here, look at these."

Claire blinked. "Kitchens? Really, Mother? Tonight? After everything, you want me to look at *kitchens*?"

"Yes, Claire. Look at kitchens," Janet said, crossing her arms. "Because your father and I are going to be paying for it. Within reason, of course."

Claire and Ryan exchanged startled looks, both stammering at the same time.

"We can't," she said.

"That's too much," Ryan said.

"And you already helped so much with the deposit," Claire added, holding the papers out.

Janet waved them back towards her. "You do what you can to look after the people you care about, even when things are rough around the edges." She patted Claire's cheek and added, "Besides, I've had a good year with the cleaning. There's money in mess, you know."

Claire paused, taking in the rare moment of her mother's unguarded warmth. For once, she was lost for words.

"And I'm sorry I was so mean about Carol," Janet admitted after clearing her throat. "I heard that Kris left her. I might go over. She could use someone, I think."

"Are you sure that's wise?" Claire asked. "She's not exactly your biggest fan."

"No," Janet admitted, fiddling with the corner of her cardigan. "But you weren't mine once either, and you gave me chance after chance. I love you, Claire. I know it's early, but Merry Christmas."

"Merry Christmas, Mum," Claire said, stepping into a hug. "And thank you for the offer. And Dad. It's really too kind." Still locked in the hug, she asked, "Please tell me you're not going to individually wrap every part of the kitchen."

"Now *there's* an idea."

Janet wandered back downstairs to join Alan for hot chocolates by the fire, and Claire and Ryan held each other in the quiet.

"What should we do?" Ryan asked, his voice low. "It's

too late for that film. We could look through these kitchens?"

"Tomorrow." Claire leaned into him, her forehead resting against his chest. "Tonight, let's brush our teeth and go to bed."

Ryan chuckled, tilting her chin up. "Your best plan yet."

Hand in hand, they left behind the papers of potential kitchens and the echo of a long, challenging year.

Tomorrow, they would move into their bare shell and begin building something together, step by step. But tonight, they had earned their rest.

"Will you take the job at the gallery?" she whispered to Ryan.

"I think so," he replied.

CHAPTER SEVENTEEN

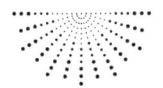

On Christmas Eve, Claire's Candles finally quietened down. The last-minute shoppers had come and gone, buying things for aunts and mothers, Secret Santa stockings and presents for teachers. Claire was content to manage the steady trickle as the rest of the village settled down for the big day.

In the end, she'd made far too many of the spiced orange candles and had still sold almost as many as last year's frosted plum scent. She'd knock a few pounds off the price, and they'd all be gone by New Year.

Lucy and Maria had been in for a while, piling their baskets high with any candle they wanted, which Claire had insisted they have free of charge.

"You really don't have to do this," Lucy said, holding a

wildflower jar to the winter light. "They're so well-crafted. It feels like an insult to take them without giving you something in return."

"Call it an apology," Claire said. "I suspected you both of murder at different points."

"That, we probably deserved," Maria said as she topped her basket up with wax melts. "Lucy is right about these being well-crafted. These scents are top-notch. I can't pick my favourites."

"Then take one of everything," Claire said. "Between you and me, I have far too much overflow stock upstairs. I think I stress-made too many candles while waiting for the building work to be finished."

"And then *we* showed up," Maria chuckled as she hoisted her full basket onto the counter. "Sorry for throwing such a spanner in the works. I can't help but wonder what would have happened if we'd picked another house."

"Jodie still would have been blackmailing people," Lucy said in a small but defiant voice. "If not here, somewhere else. The mistake came when we—or should I say, *I*—let Jodie in. I should have known she'd try and take over. That's what she always did."

"And if not Jodie, then Ricky," Maria said with a sad sigh. "I did like him. Who's to say what he would have become without Jodie's influence." Another sigh, she added, "Stuart, too. For all his faults, he was never anything but civil and respectful to us. Perhaps our biggest mistake was thinking that we could all trust each other."

"It sounded like it started out a well-intended pursuit," Claire said.

"I suppose it did," Lucy said, digging into her pocket. "But I *am* going to insist that you let me pay for at least some of these. You've already been too generous."

"Stop offering to pay the woman!" Maria muttered, reaching for a lavender candle to add to her basket. "You never have cash—" She froze mid-sentence as Lucy pulled out a crisp stack of banknotes from her pocket. "Oh, Lucy. Not *this* again. Where did you get those?"

Lucy bit back a smile, a faint blush creeping up her cheeks. "I earned it."

"How? We haven't done anything this past week except recover at the B&B from what happened the week before."

"I earned it over the past few years," Lucy said, counting out some of the notes. She handled it like it was no more real to her than Monopoly money. "Jodie and Ricky might have had their 'projects' for me, but I had one of my own." Her grin grew until it lit up her entire face in a way Claire hadn't seen before. "Something to keep me sane, but as I banked all of my work, I realised I might have a ticket out of here."

"Banked what work?" Maria raised an eyebrow. "What *are* you talking about?"

"For every fake painting I did for Jodie, I made one of my own. *Originals*. Influenced by others, but completely my style. Pure Lucy." Her tone softened, as though she were confessing something sacred. "Portraits, mainly. Jodie always had me painting landscapes, but it's faces I like. People. You have a kind face, Claire."

She peered up from under her purple fringe, still shy, but more vocal than she'd been in the short weeks Claire had known her.

"I stashed them away, one by one," she continued. "It started off to please me, but when I saw how quickly my forgeries were selling, I realised what I had. Why Jodie was so desperate to put me to work. I started to paint *my* paintings not for escape but for freedom."

"You've sold them already?" Maria asked, shaking her head in disbelief.

"The press from the case gave me a platform," she said, biting her lip from the excitement. "People started digging into who I was, what I'd done, and someone came forward and said they'd bought one of my originals at a car boot. I sold it a few years ago for twenty quid to pay for a bus from Wiltshire." She choked back a laugh. "They just sold it on for *thousands*, and suddenly, all these collectors were making offers I couldn't refuse. One by one, I sold every painting I had. They're gone. All of them."

"Lucy!" Maria gasped. "How much did you—?"

"Enough," Lucy said simply. She reached into her bag and pulled out an envelope even thicker than Carol's blackmail stash. "And this is for you."

Maria blinked at it. "For me?"

"For you," Lucy said with a giggle. "£10,000. Go off and do whatever. Start a business, travel the world—whatever you *want*. You don't have to protect me anymore. This won't change what happened, but I can finally be independent." Frowning, she added, "And maybe I always could, I just had to believe it."

Maria's lips quivered as she shook her head. "Oh, Lucy. I can't… I… It's too much."

"It's not enough," Lucy interrupted, her voice steady. "You've been my shield for years, but I'm not the person I was. I think I'm going to be okay now."

Maria swallowed hard, her hands trembling as she opened the envelope. She looked like she might throw up, but Claire was on the verge of tears.

"Do you *want* me to go?" Maria asked in a small voice.

Lucy smiled, reaching out to squeeze her hand. "Not at all. I still have one family member left."

"Oh, Lucy." Maria gave a teary laugh. "Maybe we can start fresh. A band of two."

"Three," Lucy corrected. "I've always wanted to have a cat."

"Four," Claire interjected from behind the counter, wiping away a tear. "They're better in pairs."

The three of them shared a laugh, a warm moment of relief and solidarity in the candle shop. The trials of the past few weeks—the blackmail, the murders, the betrayals—seemed to melt away, leaving behind something simpler in the air: spiced orange and hope.

"Where will you go?" Claire asked as she bagged up their candles.

"Anywhere," Lucy said, shrugging.

"Anywhere sounds good to me," Maria agreed, wrapping an arm around Lucy's shoulder. "What's that old saying? Home is where the heart is."

"You could stay in Northash?" Claire suggested. "We have plenty of heart here, when there isn't a drama unfolding on your doorstep."

"This *is* anywhere," Maria pointed out, "but I don't think it's *our* anywhere."

"No." Lucy accepted a bag across the counter. "Anywhere drama-free. I think we've earned some peace, quiet, and rest."

"I think you have," Claire agreed, walking around the counter to hug them both. "And if you ever find yourself anywhere near here, you know you've always got a friend in me."

"Thank you, Claire," Lucy said, taking the rest of her bags. "For everything."

Outside, Lucy tilted her face to the fading light as the last of the Christmas Eve sun sank below the horizon. Maria lingered, watching Lucy through the window. Both women seemed lighter now, unburdened in a way they hadn't been when Claire first met them. Maria turned back to the counter as Claire finished bagging up her candles.

"You were right," Maria said quietly, breaking the silence. "At the gallery. I did lose someone."

Claire paused, meeting Maria's gaze.

"A son," Maria continued, her gaze distant. "Marco. He was about Lucy's age when he died—he'd be about your age now."

"I'm sorry, Maria."

Maria shook her head. "Don't be sorry. Just... thank you. For seeing something in me that I'd forgotten was there."

Claire smiled gently. "Take care of each other."

Maria glanced out the window at Lucy, who was twirling in the frosty air like a child.

"Yes," Maria said, her voice unwavering. "I think we will."

She lifted her bags, her hands trembling slightly, but this time, not from exhaustion or fear. She gave Claire one last look, a small but genuine smile tugging at her lips, before stepping outside to join Lucy.

Claire watched them go, the two figures fading into the soft glow of the streetlights. She lingered at the door, her hand resting on the frame, before returning to her shop, the warmth and scent of candles wrapping around her like a comforting blanket.

CHAPTER EIGHTEEN

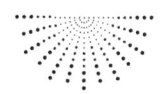

The sun peeked through the frosty windows of their new home, bathing the bare walls and unpacked boxes in bright Christmas morning light. The house wasn't perfect—far from it. The sitting room still smelled faintly of paint, the mismatched furniture looked like it had been borrowed from five different houses, and their dining table was an old door balanced on trestles. But it was theirs.

Claire perched on the edge of the sagging sofa, holding her mug of hastily reheated coffee, while Ryan set a plate of slightly burnt bacon sandwiches on the coffee table. Sid and Domino were curled upstairs on their new bed, enjoying the peace and quiet.

"Breakfast of champions," he announced, dropping beside her and draping an arm around her shoulders.

"More like breakfast of pyromaniacs," Claire teased, taking a bite. "You're lucky I love you."

"You're lucky I didn't set the fire alarm off."

Across the room, Hugo sat cross-legged on the floor, quickly unwrapping a box with Amelia hovering over his shoulder.

"It's not fair," she whined. "I want to open one now."

"You're older. You can wait," Hugo said, pulling out a new Switch game. His face lit up. "Thanks, Dad. Thanks, Claire."

Ryan grabbed a small box wrapped in lopsided paper from under their half-decorated tree.

"Go on then," he said, passing it to Amelia. "Start with this one."

Amelia squealed as she tore into it, revealing a pair of Converse shoes.

"The ones I wanted!" she shouted, holding them up like trophies. "How did you know?"

"That's because you told me six times," Claire said, grinning.

"And wrote it on the fridge," Ryan added.

"And texted me a picture," Claire finished.

The kids were soon knee-deep in wrapping paper, their laughter filling the room. Claire leaned back, savouring the mess, until Ryan nudged her with his elbow.

"Your turn," he said, handing her a large, awkwardly wrapped box.

Claire set her mug down and peeled back the paper, revealing a collection of jars, wicks, and new candle moulds.

"For your new craft room upstairs," he said. "Damon pointed me in the right direction."

"It's perfect. Thank you." Claire reached under the tree and handed him a box. "Seems we were thinking along the same lines. Here."

Ryan opened it slowly, his eyebrows lifting when he saw the art supplies—brushes, canvases, and tubes of paint neatly packed together.

"Lucy said this was the good stuff," she said.

"Oh, it is." Ryan leaned over and kissed her, his hand warm on her cheek. "Looks like we've both got projects to keep us busy."

"Get a room!" Hugo groaned, covering his eyes.

"We have a whole house," Claire said.

Amelia joined Hugo in making exaggerated gagging sounds, and Ryan threw a scrunched-up ball of wrapping paper at them.

"Watch it," he said, "or you're getting coal next year."

"Coal's cool," Hugo said. "I use it in *Minecraft*."

"And I can draw with it," Amelia pointed out.

"Well, maybe I'll swap your presents?"

"No!" they both cried.

Claire shook her head, laughing as she picked up her coffee. "Perfect first Christmas here?" she asked, leaning into Ryan's side.

"Perfect," he agreed.

The kids bickered playfully, the smell of burnt bacon lingered in the air, and the tree twinkled in its half-decorated glory. Somehow, they'd made it this far.

The chaos paused as the doorbell rang.

"Does anyone want to get that?" Claire called.

"Not it!" Amelia and Hugo yelled at the same time.

Claire pushed herself up and walked into the hallway, almost tripping over Hugo's shoes. She'd told him to line them up near the side, but she'd remind him again tomorrow; she really was turning into her mother.

She opened their new front door to find Sally standing on the doorstep, wrapped in a stylish trench coat and practically vibrating with excitement. Damon hovered behind her, looking sheepish but happy—and relieved.

"I didn't see *this* coming *at all*," Sally blurted, thrusting her hand out. A sparkling diamond ring sat on her finger, catching the winter sunlight. "We're getting married!"

"*Sally!*" Claire's eyes widened, and she pulled Sally into a hug. "Congratulations! Damon, you sly thing!"

"You knew, didn't you?" Sally whispered into her ear.

"Sort of," Claire admitted. "But he kept me in the dark for longer than he should have."

"Men." Sally rolled her eyes before winking in her new fiancé's direction. "He waited until we'd opened everything, and there was one box left waiting for me under the tree. It was so small, I didn't see it." She looked at the ring, biting into her bottom lip. "Just like my gran's."

Sally rushed inside to show off her ring, Ellie and Aria trailing behind in new matching coats. Damon followed, and he hadn't stopped smiling since she'd opened the door.

"Come here," Claire said, dragging him into a hug. "I'm proud of you, you know. You've taken a huge leap."

"We're used to huge leaps," he said, and they turned towards Warton Candle Factory on the hill—Christmas Day was one of the few days of the year it wasn't running. "Where to next?"

"Who knows?" she said, patting the scaffolding. "Exciting, no?"

"Terrifying," he replied with a laugh as a champagne cork popped inside. "Me? Married? To Sally?"

"You're not down the aisle yet," she said, pushing the door open further. "Come in, and take your shoes off. The carpet is new."

"Yes, Janet," he said.

As Sally regaled the disinterested kids with her big news, Claire caught Ryan's eye across the room. He was leaning against the back of the sofa, watching the scene with a soft smile. When their eyes met, something unspoken passed between them.

They'd discussed marriage before, agreeing it wasn't a priority. But now, watching Sally's joy and Damon's quiet pride, Claire saw something different in Ryan's expression. A thought crept into her mind. She wasn't in a white dress, but Ryan was by her side. She bit her lip and shook the thought away.

Ryan noticed and raised an eyebrow, stepping closer. "What's going on in that brain of yours?"

Claire hesitated, but the thought hadn't gone anywhere. "I'm just hearing wedding bells, that's all."

"Yeah, me too," he said, pulling her close. "Wouldn't be the worst thing, would it?"

"No," she replied. "It wouldn't."

AFTER CHRISTMAS LUNCH AT THEIR MAKESHIFT TABLE, Claire visited her neighbour with a spiced orange candle in hand. It was the one she'd planned to light as a christening for their new home—the first of the batch—but there'd be other candles. This one felt right for Carol. A simple tag dangled from the jar, scrawled in Claire's neatest handwriting: *Something to change your mind about candles. Merry Christmas. From, Next Door.*

She placed the candle on the doorstep, adjusted the

tag, and turned to leave. As she walked down the path, the door opened behind her.

"Thank you, Claire," Carol said softly, holding the candle as though it might break in her hands. Her face, usually hardened by years of suspicion and guardedness, was open now.

Claire turned back. "It's nothing."

"No, it's not." Carol's voice cracked. "I don't know how you didn't slap me."

Claire shrugged. "We're neighbours. Forgive and forget?"

"Yes." Carol exhaled slowly, her breath visible in the chilly air. "I really would like to forget this whole ordeal."

"Me too."

The sound of cheerful voices carried across the cul-de-sac. Claire turned to see her parents, Janet and Alan, dressed in their finest Santa and Mrs Claus outfits, striding across the melting snow with bright red sacks over their shoulders.

"Are you *sure* you won't come for Christmas lunch?" Janet called out, her voice as clear as a bell. "I've made enough to feed the village!"

"We've already eaten," she said, patting her full stomach. "I remembered to take it out of the freezer."

"You've never been shy of a second helping, Claire," Janet announced, glancing in Carol's direction as she lingered on the doorstep. "Have you had your Christmas lunch yet, Carol?"

"No," she replied quickly, still sniffing the candle. "I wasn't going to bother."

"Well, there's a place set at ours," Janet said, holding up a hand—and offering a bridge. "Merry Christmas."

"Thanks," Carol said, tipping the candle to them as she stepped back into her house. "I'll think about it. Merry Christmas."

When Carol softly closed the door, Janet hurried to Claire's side and whispered, "Are you *ever* going to tell me why Jodie was blackmailing her?"

"No," she replied. "Now, drop it."

Janet huffed, but she continued into 1 Birch Close with her sack of presents, putting Claire and Ryan to shame with the amount she'd bought for the grandkids.

"Merry Christmas, little one," Alan said, joining Claire on the garden path. "Do you know what you've got yourself in for, moving next to your mother?"

Claire laughed. "I guess I'm a glutton for punishment."

"This came for you and Ryan yesterday." He pulled an oblong shape from the bag and handed Claire a carefully wrapped package. "Left on our doorstep, but the instructions were clear not to open until Christmas Day."

Curious, Claire carried the present back inside. She set the present on the dining table, where Ryan was already tackling carving up the leftover turkey for sandwiches later. Amelia and Hugo were sprawled on the rug in the sitting room, ripping through the wrappings of the toys Janet had been buying and stashing in her wardrobe since early spring.

"What's that?" Ryan asked.

"I'm not sure," she said as she untied the ribbon and peeled back the paper. "But I have a feeling."

Inside was a painting of their home—not as it was, with its scaffolding and bare walls, but as it could be. A sun-drenched garden bursting with colour framed the house, and the windows seemed to sparkle with light. It had never looked like this, not even when Mrs Beaton could tend to her garden, but it could—one day.

"Ryan, look at this."

He wiped his hands on a towel and joined her, his eyes widening. "That's incredible. From Lucy?"

"Must be," she said, squinting at the signature in the corner. "It's beautiful."

"And I can get the garden looking like that in no time," Alan announced, bustling through the door with the leftover champagne flutes. "Because I've been thinking about what I'd like to plant—if you'd let me. Better to get ahead of these things…"

Claire smiled, thinking of everything that had led them to this moment. The trials, the mysteries, the chaos, and yet, here they were, together at Christmas. Home, and it still felt like they were at the very beginning.

Thank you for reading, and I hope you enjoyed an extra special visit to Northash and Claire's Candles! If you did, don't forget to leave a quick **rating/review**!

CLAIRE'S CANDLES WILL RETURN in 2025
Sign up my newsletter at AgathaFrost.com to keep up to date!

And don't forget to follow me on **Amazon**, **Facebook**, and **Instagram**!

WANT TO BE KEPT UP TO DATE WITH AGATHA FROST RELEASES? *SIGN UP THE FREE NEWSLETTER!*

www.AgathaFrost.com

You can also follow **Agatha Frost** across social media. Search 'Agatha Frost' on:

Facebook
Twitter
Goodreads
Instagram

ALSO BY AGATHA FROST

Meadowfield Bookshop (NEW)

2. The Plot Thickens

1. The Last Draft

Claire's Candles

11. Spiced Orange Suspicion

10. Double Espresso Deception

9. Frosted Plum Fears

8. Wildflower Worries

7. Candy Cane Conspiracies

6. Toffee Apple Torment

5. Fresh Linen Fraud

4. Rose Petal Revenge

3. Coconut Milk Casualty

2. Black Cherry Betrayal

1. Vanilla Bean Vengeance

Peridale Cafe

32. Lemon Drizzle Loathing

31. Sangria and Secrets

30. **Mince Pies and Madness**

29. **Pumpkins and Peril**

28. **Eton Mess and Enemies**

27. **Banana Bread and Betrayal**

26. **Carrot Cake and Concern**

25. **Marshmallows and Memories**

24. **Popcorn and Panic**

23. **Raspberry Lemonade and Ruin**

22. **Scones and Scandal**

21. **Profiteroles and Poison**

20. **Cocktails and Cowardice**

19. **Brownies and Bloodshed**

18. **Cheesecake and Confusion**

17. **Vegetables and Vengeance**

16. **Red Velvet and Revenge**

15. **Wedding Cake and Woes**

14. **Champagne and Catastrophes**

13. **Ice Cream and Incidents**

12. **Blueberry Muffins and Misfortune**

11. **Cupcakes and Casualties**

10. **Gingerbread and Ghosts**

9. **Birthday Cake and Bodies**

8. **Fruit Cake and Fear**

7. Macarons and Mayhem

6. Espresso and Evil

5. Shortbread and Sorrow

4. Chocolate Cake and Chaos

3. Doughnuts and Deception

2. Lemonade and Lies

1. Pancakes and Corpses

Other

The Agatha Frost Winter Anthology

Peridale Cafe Book 1-10

Peridale Cafe Book 11-20

Claire's Candles Book 1-3

Printed in Great Britain
by Amazon